ONCE UPON AN
APPLE

A
SNOW WHITE
RETELLING

GABRIELLE LANDI

Once Upon An Apple

Paperback Cover Design by GetCovers.
Hardcover Cover Art and Design by Ireen Chau.
Character Art by Ireen Chau.
Editing by Lisa Henson.
Map by Cartographybird Maps.

ISBNs:
Hardcover: 979-8-9865460-8-7
Paperback: 979-8-9865460-9-4

CONTENTS

THE GREAT NATION OF
GALAMÈRE
AND
SURROUNDING LANDS

TO THE UNCHARTED NORTH

ELARU

THE NORTHLANDS

RIVEL

GALAMÈRE

DELTHU

TO THE SOUTHERN NATIONS

Chapter One
Sophia

There was a stranger in her barn, and he was watching her.

Sophia set down the bucket of water and turned back to the barn door, but he was gone, almost like he hadn't been there in the first place.

But she knew he'd been there.

Sophia didn't like strangers. She didn't like anyone watching her, whether she knew them or not, but strangers made her eyes twitch and a chill run down her spine.

She turned back to her goats and put the bucket of water inside the pen, water sloshing as she set it down.

"Are you ready for me to go to town?" she asked the goats as she tied the bucket to the fence. Hopefully tying it would prevent them from knocking it over before she came back.

Although Ivy had a way of knocking over just about everything, whether it was tied down or not. But maybe this time she would come back from town to a full bucket of water and not a puddle on the floor.

Mollie came bounding over and rubbed her head against Sophia's hand. Sophia smiled and rubbed the little goat's chin.

Mollie was her favorite. The goats technically weren't hers—they belonged to Lord and Lady Rendon, or more specifically, their young daughter Liliana. But since Liliana did nothing but play with them on occasion, they were effectively Sophia's goats.

Even though Liliana had named the other three babies, Sophia had named Mollie, and she loved the little goat with all her heart.

"I'll be back to check on you later," she told Mollie. She was going to go to town, spend some time at the café with her friends, and avoid any strange men.

Sophia grabbed her shawl from where she'd put it on the hook by the door and started walking to town. As she walked through the gates of the manor, she looked back at it and smiled. Her new home had been wonderful to her. Such a difference from when she lived with Lady Manning. The freedom was intoxicating, and she couldn't ever imagine going back to her old home, if it could even be called that.

The last thing she wanted was a strange man hovering around it.

The short walk to town felt longer than usual, her senses on high alert as she watched for any strangers along the path. She listened to the birds singing and took in the bright colors of fall as she watched and listened for anyone who might be following her.

The orange and red hues of the trees were so different from the spring flowers that had begun to bloom shortly after she arrived in the Northlands—but it was still beautiful.

The town came into sight as she crested a hill. She quickened her pace and made her way to the center of town, where her friend Thea owned the café.

When she opened the café door, a bell rang out. Sophia took a deep breath as she entered the café that felt like a second home to her.

There was a fire crackling in the fireplace, and the air smelled of warm, comforting foods. It wasn't easy to tell what Thea was cooking, but whatever it was, it was sure to be delicious.

Sophia scanned the café until she found Ginger, the resident cat of the Cozy Cat Café, and wandered over to scratch under her chin for a moment. Ginger started purring almost immediately, and after a moment, Sophia gave her a pat on the head and made her way to the counter.

Thea waited with a smile, her face lighting up when Sophia approached. Today she wore a green apron that set off her dark brown skin.

Sophia inspected it as she approached. Was that a kitten embroidered on the top?

It was.

"Hello," Thea said warmly. "How are you today?"

"I'm well," Sophia said. She was still uneasy over the stranger, though being here had washed away most of the anxiety. This place was a soothing balm for her soul.

Thea narrowed her eyes, her fingers drumming a rhythm against the counter. "What happened?"

Sophia shrugged her shoulders, her feet fidgeting. "Nothing much."

Thea reached out to place her hand over Sophia's. "I can tell something's not right."

Sophia wasn't used to having someone be concerned for her feelings. It was nice, even if she didn't want to answer the question.

She chewed on her bottom lip as the bell over the door rang again. Their friend Dietrich walked in, conveniently saving her from having to answer.

"Hello, friends," he said as he made his way to the counter. "How are you today?"

"Something happened to Sophia, and she won't tell me what's wrong," Thea said.

"Thea," Sophia hissed.

She shouldn't have assumed Dietrich's presence would save her, but she didn't expect Thea to tell Dietrich that something was wrong.

Dietrich's eyes widened as he turned to Sophia. "What happened?"

"Nothing's wrong," Sophia protested.

Dietrich threw an arm around her shoulders, his dark brown hair flopping over his forehead with the motion. "If you think I'm going to take no for an answer after saving your life, then something is definitely wrong with you."

Dietrich's concern made something well up in her throat.

He and Thea were her first friends, and the fact that they were worried about her made her want to cry, which was unusual. But showing emotion always led to future trouble, so she shoved it down and shook her head. "Honestly, it's nothing. There was a stranger in the barn earlier and I overreacted."

Across the counter, Thea frowned. "There aren't many strangers around these parts."

"I'm sure I just didn't recognize him since I'm so new. It rattled me a little, that's all. I don't like strangers."

Anything to convince them to stop asking her questions.

Sophia didn't like being the center of attention.

"And yet you moved to a town full of strangers," Dietrich said with an easy grin. "I'll take my regular, Thea, and I'll get the goat girl's drink, too."

"I can get my own," Sophia protested. "I make enough money."

Dietrich grinned. "Yeah, but sometimes it's fun to throw you for a loop."

Sophia sighed as Dietrich paid for both of their drinks. "You didn't have to do that. Let me—"

"You know he's not gonna let you pay it back," Thea said as she bustled away to make their drinks, "so don't even bother trying."

"I was going to get my own drink," Sophia said weakly as Dietrich ushered her over to the cozy seats where they usually sat.

Ginger was curled up next to Sophia's usual chair, waiting. As Sophia settled into her seat, the orange cat made her way onto her lap, purring in anticipation. Sophia leaned down and gave her a hug before petting her gently.

"So other than the stranger, anything else happening this week?" Dietrich asked, taking up most of a double occupant seat as he sprawled back. He ran his fingers through his hair and looked over at Sophia. "Are the goats giving you more trouble?"

"Always," she said. "Especially little Mollie. She has a way of getting out and getting into everything constantly."

"And yet she's your favorite somehow." Dietrich said, rolling his eyes.

"I know," Sophia said with a smile. "She's just too cute. I just love her little brown nose and the white spot on her forehead."

"She's got you totally taken in," Dietrich said. "You love every moment of it and she's not even your goat."

Sophia shrugged. "It's not like Liliana is out there that often. She's basically mine."

"Sounds like an awful lot of trouble for your weekly wages," Dietrich said.

"At least I get weekly wages."

He frowned and sat up straight. "What do you mean, at least you get weekly wages? Did you not get paid at your last place?"

Sophia shook her head. She shouldn't have brought it up. She didn't want to talk about it, and now Dietrich wasn't going to let it go.

Dietrich was an odd case. He liked to circumvent the rules sometimes, and yet he had an innate sense of justice that she'd rarely seen in the world, which was rather inconvenient when she made the mistake of bringing up her past.

"Where were you that you didn't get paid?" Dietrich asked. "I'm pretty sure that's illegal."

Sophia huffed. "I don't think she cared. There's a reason I left."

She didn't want to think about it. In fact, she'd be more than happy to pretend it had never happened in the first place.

"The past is the past," she said as Thea arrived with their drinks in hand. Sophia took hers with a murmured "thank you" as Thea sat down across from them.

"What's in the past?" Thea asked, perching primly on the edge of her seat, always ready to jump up at a moment's notice if something was needed.

Sophia took the first sip of her cinnamon honey coffee and relaxed, the drink soothing her somewhat.

"Sophia's not telling us everything about her previous occupation," Dietrich said. "But since I don't particularly want you all digging around in my past, either, I think I'm going to let it go."

Sophia tucked that nugget of information away. What was in Dietrich's past that was so bad? She knew that he'd lived in Riyel for many years, only coming back somewhat recently.

Did he have bad memories of Riyel, too?

He took a sip of his drink and sighed happily, relaxing back into the seat as he brushed his hair out of his eyes. "Great job as always, Thea. You are a master at crafting the perfect beverage."

Thea smiled. "It's all my father's recipes."

"And your hard work," Sophia said with a smile, hoping to at least pretend that she wasn't as rattled as she was.

What if the man had been sent by Lady Manning to find her? Thea was right. Strangers weren't common around here.

She took a deep breath as the bell over the door rang again and Beatrice walked in.

Thea jumped to her feet and hurried behind the counter.

"I need a drink really quickly, and then I have to get back," Beatrice said, pausing at their chairs to give Sophia a hug from behind, the back of the chair between them digging into Sophia's neck as she tried to lean into Beatrice's hug.

"What are they working you to death for?" Dietrich asked. "It's just a bunch of books. How important can they really be?"

"For the sake of our friendship, I'm going to forget you said that." Beatrice thumped him on the back of his head as she walked past to pay for her drink.

"Better not insult her books," Sophia told Dietrich. "You know how important they are to her."

"Just as important as your goats are to you," he said.

Sophia put her nose in the air and adopted a haughty accent. "Absolutely," she said in her best mimicry of Lady Manning.

Not that she didn't like books, but her goats were definitely better.

Books couldn't snuggle you the way Mollie did.

"Just remember," Dietrich warned. "They're not your goats. It's one thing to love them, but we aren't nobility and it's best not to get too attached to things."

Why did he look so shifty all of a sudden? What had he gotten attached to in the past that he'd lost?

Beatrice hurried over and sat down next to Sophia, putting her arm around her for a half hug. Her long brown hair brushed against Sophia's neck as she reached over to pet Ginger, who was still perched on Sophia's lap. "I need a better hug. Today has been so busy," she said. "So far, I've helped at least four children finish their schoolwork, the blacksmith needed information on one of the laws—"

"What law?" Dietrich asked, leaning forward with interest.

Beatrice shook her head. "You know I can't tell you that," she said. "If I told everyone's secrets, no one would come to the library anymore."

Dietrich shrugged. "Pretty sure they can figure it out without the library, anyway."

"Dietrich," Sophia said in a warning tone. "If you two start going at it, I'm going to leave. Apologize."

He sighed. "I'm sorry, that was unkind to you. Please forgive me."

"Only if you come pick out a book to read," Beatrice said, a wicked glint in her eye.

Dietrich shuddered. "Maybe I'm not that sorry."

Beatrice laughed. "I was only teasing you. But don't forget, the library is always there if you need anything."

Dietrich shook his head. "Not likely."

"I know," Beatrice said with a smile as she stood. "I'll be there nonetheless."

Thea arrived with a steaming mug for Beatrice. "Just bring it back before you go home for the night," she said, handing it over along with a wrapped muffin. "And here's this. I imagine you probably forgot lunch again, didn't you?"

Beatrice grinned. "You're the best, Thea."

"I know," Thea said with a wink as Beatrice rushed off again, back to the library.

Thea mothered everyone who came to the café. It was one of Sophia's favorite things about visiting her.

Sophia stayed a while longer, chatting with Dietrich, Thea, and a few other friends who came and went. Her days off rarely aligned with everyone's, but she had come to love everyone she'd met at the Cozy Cat Café, and loved seeing any of them who were able to pop in on her day off.

All too soon, it was time to head for home.

"Here, dear, have a muffin," Thea said, hurrying behind the counter. "I think I made too many."

Thea made too many muffins on purpose, she was sure of it. And yet, she couldn't resist taking it. She breathed in the scent of the spicy, pumpkin-y muffin and closed her eyes in a moment of pure happiness. "Thank you," she said.

"Just a little treat," Thea said with a wink.

Sophia wrapped her shawl around her shoulders as she let herself out the door. The breeze was cool, but her shawl kept her warm as she ate her muffin on the walk home.

She kept an eye out for the stranger, but there was no sight of him.

Maybe he was just passing through.

Maybe she was overreacting.

She made her way to the kitchen for some bread and cheese, eating it as she prepared for bed, and settled on the cot in the room that she shared with some of the other maids.

"Did you see that new guard?" one of the girls asked.

"I heard he's just arrived from Riyel," another said.

"He's so handsome," a third said.

Sophia kept her head down. She didn't want to draw attention to herself, and she didn't like gossiping—though she didn't mind listening to it.

A handsome new guard seemed like an apt description for the stranger in the barn, which was some comfort. It didn't change her mind, though.

The other girls could stare all they wanted.

She would avoid the stranger.

Chapter Two
CASPIAN

CASPIAN WALKED IN THE door of his parents' home, and his heart swelled in relief. He was finally back home. Training to be a guard in Riyel for the past two years had been a good experience, but there was nothing like being home with family.

He stepped into his mother's sitting room, and there was a cry of delight when his little sister Liliana saw him. She rushed at him and jumped as she threw her arms around his neck, holding on for dear life as he swung her around.

"Caspian," she shrieked, her long golden hair brushing against his skin. "You're here!" She giggled as he tickled her in an effort to loosen her arms from around his neck. "I thought you'd never come home."

"Of course I was going to come home," he told her.

"You missed my birthday," she informed him, pouting.

"That's right, I did. Happy birthday. How old are you now, five?"

Liliana gasped. "I'm eight years old. Five is a baby."

She would always be a baby to him, but he refrained from saying that.

His mother had hurried over to give him a hug. "I didn't know you were coming back so early," she said. "I would have gotten everything ready for you."

"I don't need everything ready for me, Mother," he said with a laugh. "I've been roughing it for two years. Anything you have is more than enough for me right now."

Lady Rendon laughed. "I can imagine. Truthfully, it's far harder to imagine you, of all my children, roughing it."

Caspian grimaced. "To be fair, I have gotten better, but you're right. My dislike of dirt does mean I got good marks for keeping my armor and sword clean, though."

"I should hope you get good marks for more than that," his mother teased before turning to his sister. "Liliana, go get your father and tell him that your brother has come home."

Liliana slid down Caspian's side and ran off to their father's study, and Lady Rendon gave Caspian another fierce hug. "We've missed you so much around here," his mother said, squeezing him tightly.

Caspian took in his mother's floral scent and the bright and warm decor of her sitting room and felt peace run through his soul. Being home was good for him. It would give him the right frame of mind to make the decision that he had to make.

His sister came running back, his father and oldest brother following her, and emotion welled up in him at the sight of them. He shoved it down, though. Being emotional was a weakness in the Guard. He'd had plenty of practice in avoiding emotions the past two years.

"Caspian, my boy," his father said, sweeping him into a hug.

Though Caspian was the youngest of the three boys, he was the tallest, and dwarfed even his father. But there was nothing like a hug from his father to make him feel like he was a child again.

Even two years of experience in the Royal Guard couldn't change that.

"I thought you weren't getting home until next week," his brother said when it was his turn for a hug, clapping Caspian on the back.

"Let us out early," Caspian said. "We're not sure why, but nobody waited long enough to ask."

"I can imagine. Eager to get home to your families, I bet."

"Exactly," Caspian said. "Even to the annoying brothers who got to stay home instead of being shipped off to learn how to be a guard."

Kellan laughed again. "Hey, it's not my fault I'm the oldest. I would have switched with you, you know that."

Caspian did know that, which is why he didn't resent his brother.

It would have been easier had the tables been turned. Kellan had little interest in being a lord, though he always would be, and Caspian had always leaned toward the business of running an estate. But he had an aversion to the idea of finding a wealthy woman to marry simply to gain an estate of his own, so he'd gone off to the Guard.

"Are you ready for dinner?" his mother asked from where she stood next to his father, his arm wrapped around her waist. They'd always been in love, one of the reasons that marrying for wealth and status seemed rather distasteful. It was hard to imagine marriage for political reasons when he'd seen what a true marriage could be.

"Have I ever not been ready for food?" Caspian said with an easy grin as Liliana raced forward and captured his hand with hers. "Of course I'm ready for dinner. What do you think we're having tonight?"

"I'm sure it will be something you love," Lady Rendon said.

"That's because I love all the food we eat here," he said with a grin. "It's much better than the grub in the barracks."

"I can't imagine why," his brother said with a wry smile as they made their way down to the dining room.

It wasn't as if Caspian had been solely focused on arriving home in time for dinner...but he might have done his best to leave early enough to make it in time. Even if that required an earlier wake-up than he'd wanted.

It was all worth it when he walked into the dining room and saw the food laid out on the table, the smell of a home-cooked meal filling him with nostalgia and anticipation. "It's almost like Cook knew I was coming home," he said, taking in the roast chicken, mashed potatoes, roasted vegetables, and more that covered the table. "This is a bounty."

"Just for you, my darling," his mother said as she walked past him toward her seat.

Lord Rendon leaped into action, pulling out his wife's seat with a proud smile.

"Thank you, my love," his mother said.

Caspian smiled at his parents. He wanted a love like theirs—though where he was going to find it, he wasn't sure. Women weren't exactly lining up to marry one of the king's guards, even if he was nobility. But his parents had been an example of true love for most of his life, and he couldn't wait to find a love like theirs.

Maybe then, he would finally be the best thing in someone's life. Not just one of three brothers, of four children, of a thousand guards, but the best thing in someone's life.

He sat down next to his sister as his other brother came in, his footsteps loud against the wooden floor.

He was home for once. That was a surprise.

"Caspian," Gideon exclaimed, rushing over and grabbing him in a hug from behind. "What are you doing here, you sorry sight for sore eyes?"

Caspian grinned and clapped his brother's shoulder. "Couldn't wait to get back to Mother and Liliana," he said. "Could've avoided you, though."

"I'm wounded," Gideon said with a grin as he sat down next to Caspian, and they began serving themselves from the platters of food laid across the table.

His mother had long since insisted that when it was only the family, they were not to be served, instead asking the servants to lay out the food for them to serve themselves. It was more private, and the family enjoyed eating by themselves without servants constantly bustling around.

Caspian enjoyed the time with his family where he could just be himself, instead of feeling like he had to represent the Rendon family, even to the servants in their home.

"So what is your plan, Caspian?" his oldest brother asked. "Do you plan to stick around for a while? Or are you just here for a week?"

Caspian shrugged. "We don't have to let them know if we're coming back for a couple of months, so I have time to wait and see what I want to do. For now, I plan to get fat and lazy."

"On Father's dime?" his brother suggested with a smirk.

"Absolutely. What's the point of going home to visit your parents if you don't take full advantage?"

Liliana grabbed his sleeve. "Will you spend time with me while you're here?" she asked.

He smiled down at his little sister. She was a complete surprise, nearly fifteen years his junior, and was absolutely spoiled, loved, and adored.

"Of course I will," he said, smiling down at her. "You can't expect me not to spend time with my favorite sister while I'm in town."

She giggled. "I'm your only sister."

"That you know about," he said. "Didn't Mother and Father tell you about the secret sister that we have?"

Lady Rendon shook her head. "Don't lie to your sister, Caspian. She'll probably think you're telling the truth."

"It would be fun to have a sister," Liliana said with a big grin.

"That's not happening, sweetheart. You are more than enough trouble for all of us combined." Lord Rendon shook his fork at his youngest, a merry gleam in his eyes.

"I'm not trouble," Liliana retorted, "I'm perfect. You always tell me that."

Everyone laughed, and Caspian reached over and ruffled his sister's hair. "Yes, you are, Little Bit," he said. "Yes, you are."

He dug back into his food but had only managed a few more bites before his father turned to him.

"Since you're home for the next couple of months," he said, "I have a job for you. Two, actually."

Everyone looked up to hear what Lord Rendon had to say.

"You know how your mother sponsors the Fall Festival in the town every year? I want you to take it over this year. Your mother could use a break and I could use some time with her."

Lady Rendon looked like she wanted to argue, but she didn't say anything.

"I just want to spend some time with my wife," his father said to her. "Is that so wrong of me?"

His mother smiled. "No, I suppose not."

"And now that Kellan is taking over many of my duties, I actually have some time to spend with you," Lord Rendon said to his wife.

"And me?" Liliana asked eagerly.

"Of course," Lord Rendon replied. "I have plenty of time to spend with my two best girls."

"How about your best boys?" Gideon asked with a chuckle.

"Yeah, don't you want to spend time with us, too?" Caspian asked.

"I spent more than enough time chasing you boys," his father said with a grin. "I'd like to focus on my girls for a little while now."

It was true, he'd spent more than enough time chasing them around when they were younger. Quality time with their father had never been lacking, even when he was busy. Looking back, Caspian wasn't sure how his father had managed so much time with them, but he appreciated it all the more.

"I suppose we can allow that," Kellan said, fixing a pretend glare on their little sister. "You better take advantage of all this time with Father. You hear me?"

She giggled. "Of course I will. What do we get to do first?"

"Hold your horses, Little Bit," Lord Rendon said with a laugh. "Let's get your brother settled first. Caspian? Will you take over the Fall Festival for your mother?"

Caspian nodded. Taking over the Fall Festival wasn't exactly at the top of the list of things he'd hoped to do once he got home, but if it meant that his mother and sister were happy, he would do just about anything.

And it would be nice to get into town a little more. He'd been largely disconnected from the town when he grew up, something he'd wanted to change for a while but wasn't sure how best to do it.

His father had just given him the perfect reason.

Even if it wasn't the reason he would have chosen himself.

"Mother, you'll have to give me some tips. I don't know the first thing about organizing a festival."

His mother smiled. "Don't worry, dear. We have lots of wonderful connections to help. You'll want to talk to Beatrice at the library. She's been my biggest help so far."

Caspian sighed. How had he gone from swinging a sword to spending time in the library in less than two days? "And the other task?" he asked his father.

"I want you to train our guard here," Lord Rendon said. "You have more training now than any of them."

He nodded. At least that was something he felt confident in.

Being home was completely different than being an officer of the king's guard in the capital city. He would have to focus on enjoying life here as much as he could, before making the decision on what he was going to do with the rest of his life.

Training as a guard had set him up for a potential future career. He now had the next two months to decide if that's what he was going to do for the rest of his life, or if he was going to find another path.

Would planning the Fall Festival help with that decision? It didn't seem likely. But if that's what needed to happen here, then he would step up and do it.

Maybe he could become the best at planning the Fall Festival.

That surely would help his future, right?

CHAPTER THREE
SOPHIA

SOPHIA STIRRED THE SOAP in the pot, waiting for it to reach the silky-smooth consistency necessary before she could pour it into the wooden mold one of the stable hands had made for her.

She'd added a lavender essential oil to this batch, along with the extra goat milk that the goats gave her.

One of the maids at Lady Manning's had taught her how to make the soap when she was younger, though they hadn't had any goat milk there. Lady Manning abhorred animals of any kind, which made sense, since none of them liked her, either.

When she'd noticed there was extra goat milk going to waste here at the manor, Sophia had decided to try using it instead of water in a batch of soap.

It had been the best batch she'd ever made.

Of course, when a few other people had tried it, soapmaking had been added to her list of duties for the estate.

The housekeeper had mentioned that she could also sell it at the Fall Festival, at the manor's booth. She wasn't sure what or when the Fall Festival was, but she had an idea that it was coming up quickly, which meant she had to get the soap aging before she ran out of time.

Sophia watched and waited and stirred, and eventually the soap thickened and she poured it into the wooden mold. She swirled the top to make it look pretty. It wasn't a necessary step, but it made her happy to do it. And in her humble opinion, being pretty was just as important as being good soap.

She set the mold to the side so the soap could continue to harden until she unmolded it the next day.

The kitchen staff was cleaning up from lunch and was just about done as she started cleaning up her mess. She had to wash her bowls, put away the oils, and clean the bucket the milk had been in. Nothing much, but Cook would get cranky if she left a mess.

As the kitchen staff finished their chores and filtered out to take their afternoon break before beginning to prep dinner, Sophia began to hum to herself. She didn't mind the kitchen staff, but she was happiest alone in the kitchen with no one to bother her.

Maybe it was because when she lived with Lady Manning, nobody was nice to her except Rosaleen.

Here, everyone was nice enough...but she wasn't used to talking to people and didn't want to draw attention to herself. It was easier to fade into the background and avoid getting close.

She was washing up the last things when the kitchen door opened, and the stranger came in. She jumped, grabbing a dishcloth and holding it to her chest.

Because of course that would protect her from the stranger.

Why did he have to wait until everyone else left before coming into the kitchen?

Hadn't the other girls said he was a guard? The guards had all had their lunch. Why was he here?

"Hello," he said. "I'm Caspian."

Well, he'd introduced himself. Maybe he didn't have nefarious intentions.

But she still didn't want to be alone with him.

"I'm Sophia," she said quietly, picking up the wooden spoon that she had used to stir the soap. Maybe if he tried anything, the spoon would be more effective as a weapon.

Although it would be useless against the sword that was strapped around his waist.

If anything, though, the sword made her a little easier. The other girls must have been right, and he was a new guard hired by Lord Rendon.

"I won't hurt you," he said with an easy smile, taking in the way she held the spoon. "I just came to see if there was anything to eat."

"You missed lunch," Sophia said. "And Cook gets cranky if we're snacking between meals."

He grinned. "I'm sure she won't mind if I steal a little something."

"You clearly haven't met Cook," Sophia said. "She gets cranky over everything."

Caspian prowled over to the basket in the corner where the rolls they'd baked this morning were sitting. He picked one up and stared at it. "I don't suppose you know where I could find something to put on this?"

Sophia eyed him. "I just made some butter this morning. Would you like some?"

Caspian's eyes lit up. "Fresh butter on a homemade roll? Absolutely."

He smiled as she pulled the butter out from the crock in the corner where she kept it.

Most of the manor's butter came from the cows they kept...but there was something special about the butter she made with the goat milk.

Ivy had more cream in her milk than the other does, and it tended to separate out, so she always milked her into a separate pail to make butter. Maybe it was the hours of work it took to make butter that made it taste so wonderful to her, or maybe it was just that good.

But there was something about taking the grumpiest goat's milk to make her favorite thing that made taking care of Ivy just a little easier.

Caspian slathered butter onto the roll before looking around the kitchen furtively.

"I don't suppose you want to be caught with the roll," Sophia said.

"Not really," he admitted. "Just let me wash this knife—unless, of course, you want a roll, too."

Sophia shook her head. "I know better than to take food between meals."

Caspian grinned. "But you want one, don't you?"

Sophia's mouth was watering. The fresh roll and the butter looked absolutely delicious. Of course she wanted one. "I suppose I could try one, but we better hurry."

She didn't want to get in trouble with Cook for this stranger's shenanigans, but she didn't want to be left out, either.

"Of course," Caspian said, already pulling out another roll and buttering it for her. He quickly washed the knife and put it away while Sophia put the butter back and eyed him.

The other girls had been right. He was handsome.

His dark hair was cut close to his head, the way many of the guards wore it, and his beard made his face harder to see—but it made his smile all the more obvious.

"Come on, let's take these outside. We're less likely to get caught that way." He grabbed her hand and pulled her toward the outer door.

Sophia yanked her hand out of his but followed him out the door.

She felt a little less wary about him now that he'd introduced himself and offered her food, but she wasn't going to let him hold her hand.

She wouldn't mind letting him follow her to the barn, though. "I was going to go check on the goats," she said. "Want to come with me?"

The fastest way to the goats was through the barn and over a fence. She'd never climbed the fence while holding a roll before, but it couldn't be that difficult.

"Where are you going?" Caspian asked as she entered the barn.

"Going to check on the goats," she said, frowning at him. Hadn't she already said that? He was the one following her.

"You're going into the barn with food?" he asked, his nose wrinkling.

"I was going to," she said slowly, and it was almost a question. "Do you not eat in the barn?"

Caspian grimaced. "No, that does not rank up there in things I enjoy doing. I prefer to keep food and manure separate."

Sophia laughed. "I don't roll my food around in the manure," she began.

He shook his head. "Even being in the barn is too close for me. I'll just finish this out here."

Sophia leaned against the wall of the barn. "If that's what you want to do." She ate another bite. "I don't mind eating in the barn. But I spend a lot of time with the goats, I suppose."

Sure, the goats were a little dirty, but they were animals. That was part of dealing with animals.

And that's what baths were for.

But it wasn't like you were rolling your food in manure if you walked into the barn while eating.

As they finished their rolls, Sophia nodded. "Ready to meet the goats now?" she asked.

Caspian nodded. "If I must."

Sophia narrowed her eyes at him. "You don't have to if you don't want to. I was just offering. I don't suppose you need to follow me around."

He didn't have to come with her. She could have gone and checked on the goats already if she hadn't been waiting for him.

Caspian grimaced. "I'm sorry. I'm not being very good company, am I?"

That was putting it nicely. "I'll just get back to work," Sophia said, edging toward the barn. "If you want to come, you can, but I'm sure you have better things to do with your time than meet the goats if you don't like being in the barn."

Sophia entered the barn. If he wanted to, he would follow, and if not, it wasn't her problem. She didn't care either way.

She didn't have to be nice to the guard.

The goats were her job. Being nice to men wasn't.

The familiar smell of earth and animals filled her nose as she hiked up her skirt and climbed over the fence into the goat pen, jumping from the top to land just to the side of a pile of goat poop.

See, it was perfectly easy to stay clean. There was no reason to avoid silly things like eating a roll in the goat pen.

She made her way through the stall and through the outer door to see the goats in their pen outside. It wasn't a large pen, but it was enough for them to get some sunshine and fresh air.

The goats came running when they saw her, bleating loudly. No doubt they expected her to have food.

"I don't have anything for you," she said with a laugh as they ran toward her at top speed.

Mollie led the pack, jumping to put her front legs on Sophia. Sophia smiled as she gently set Mollie back down on the ground. She didn't need Mollie jumping on Liliana and knocking her over, and the sooner the baby goat learned not to jump on people, the better.

"How are you doing?" Sophia asked, rubbing Mollie's head. "I don't suppose you all dumped your water, did you?" She stared at Ivy, the most likely candidate.

But when she looked down to the end of the pen, where the stable hands had placed full buckets of water earlier in the day, their water bucket was still upright.

"You haven't knocked it over yet," she said in wonder, staring at Ivy. "I guess you must not be trying hard enough."

The bottom of the gate scraped against the fence as Caspian opened and shut it.

"Do they always knock over their bucket?"

"You followed me," she said, a little surprised. She hadn't expected him to actually follow her.

"What can I say? I couldn't let a girl be braver than I was," he said in a teasing tone, but there was some emotion in his voice that led her to believe maybe that was the only reason he was standing in her goat pen.

"Is that how it is?" Sophia said, mimicking his grin.

"Well, if the truth got out about me, I'd never live it down," he said. "It's hard enough being a guard without people thinking you can't even walk into a goat pen."

"I can see how that would be tough." Sophia nodded her head. "It must be awfully tough being a guard and not wanting to touch your own horse."

He grinned. "I don't mind my horse, but I grew up with horses. I didn't grow up with goats."

Sophia shook her head. "How you don't mind horses, but you don't like goats, I have no idea. Goat poop is way easier to deal with than horse poop."

Caspian took a tiny step back as one of the babies skittered closer to him. "And I'm just wondering how I managed to get on the topic of manure with the prettiest girl I've ever met at Rendon Manor."

His blatant flirting made Sophia blush, so she ignored it. "It's part of my life," she said, "so it's a topic I can converse about easily."

Meadow eyed the stranger warily from across the yard, while Valley brushed up against her side before sneezing all over her. Caspian edged sideways, away from the goat. "I don't suppose you have any other topics that you like talking about?" Sophia asked as she bent over to pet Tack and Ned, Ivy's twin boys.

"We could talk about many topics," Caspian said, "as long as we talk about them outside the goat pen."

Sophia laughed and made her way back into the barn, Mollie and the twins chasing her while the last baby goat, Terra, found a corner to snooze in. As she picked up her skirts to climb over the fence, Caspian opened the gate.

"Don't let the goats out," she warned.

Sensing freedom was close at hand, the goats rushed toward Caspian, who quickly shut the gate. He stared at the fence. "I see now why you climbed it earlier."

Sophia chuckled. "Yes, an open gate is pretty much an invitation for the goats to get out. It's much easier to climb the fence." She began to climb and swung her leg over the top rail, hoping that Caspian was gentleman enough not to look before her skirt settled back into place as she climbed out on the other side.

He followed suit and followed her out of the barn. "I have to go," he said, "but I hope I'll see you around the manor."

Sophia smiled as she brushed her hand along the wall of the barn. "That would be lovely."

Caspian strode away and she watched him leave, then turned back to the barn. It was almost time to feed the goats.

It would be nice to have someone to talk to.

It certainly didn't hurt that he was pleasant to look at, too.

Maybe she didn't need to stay away from him. Maybe her suspicions were just paranoia, and she could forget about her past.

Maybe, just maybe, he was someone who could see the real Sophia.

Chapter Four
CASPIAN

CASPIAN WAS GROWING MORE confused by the second after talking to his mother about her expectations for the Fall Festival.

He'd thought that maybe he had a handle on things, but the more he thought it over, the more confused he was.

So he was on his way to the town to talk to Beatrice, the librarian who supposedly ran everything.

That was part of the confusion. He had assumed his mother did all the work, but that didn't seem to be the case. It seemed their family provided money and support for the Fall Festival, while Beatrice the librarian did much of the work—with her help, his mother claimed. But what exactly his mother did, he still wasn't sure.

So he was on his way to talk to Beatrice.

It had absolutely nothing to do with the fact that he'd spotted a dark-haired young lady walking toward the town that afternoon.

Nothing to do with the fact that he hoped he would bump into her, and maybe even get to walk her back to the manor.

There was something intriguing about Sophia. Caspian wasn't sure where things might be going with her, but he definitely wanted to spend more time with her.

So here he was, on his way to the town, wondering if he could walk fast enough to catch up to her before she got there, and he lost track of her.

What did she even do in the town? Why did she leave the manor?

His thoughts tumbled around in his head as he made his way into town. Walking through the town square, he noticed the dark-haired miss sitting in the window of the Cozy Cat Café.

So that's where she was.

But then he noticed the man sitting next to her.

Was she already taken?

She'd flirted back when he'd been with her in the goat pen yesterday.

He might have flirted a little more, but he'd mostly been concerned with getting out of the goat pen without his shoes landing in goat poop or a goat jumping up on him and smearing him with mud and manure.

Of course, the prettiest girl that he'd ever seen had to be one who was in love with farm animals. She probably got along great with his sister. Liliana had talked his ear off nonstop about the goats during dinner last night.

Maybe the goats would help him have a better relationship with his sister.

And maybe having a better relationship with his sister would make him look better for the goat girl.

Not that he should be calling Sophia the goat girl. But it seemed like an obvious nickname given the way she was in love with her goats. It was clear how much she loved them, and how much they loved her back.

He made his way to the library on the other side of the square and pushed open the heavy wooden door. The library was new since he'd moved to Riyel, and he wasn't sure what to expect.

The smell of books filled the air, and he was greeted by a smiling librarian, perched on a stool, with a pencil behind her ear and a book on her lap.

"Hello," she chirped. "I'm Beatrice, how can I help you today?"

"I'm actually here to talk to you," he said, smiling at her. "I'm Caspian Rendon and I'm here to help with the Fall Festival instead of my mother, Lady Rendon."

"Oh, Caspian, I didn't recognize you with that beard."

He narrowed his eyes at the woman in front of him. She looked familiar. But why?

"You probably don't remember me," she added. "You spent most of your time with Percival when you were in town. I should probably call you Lord Caspian now that we're adults, though."

He waved his hand at her. "No need, Beatrice."

The librarian smiled. "I would love to chat with you about the festival. Come back to my office and let me pull out my plan so far. Your mother has already helped me get started, but there's plenty of work still to do."

Caspian followed her to her office at the back of the library and she pulled out a large folder with stacks of paper inside from a shelf as she passed it, clasping it to her chest as she approached her desk.

"That seems like a lot," he said, his eyes opening wide in alarm. "How much work is involved in putting together the festival?"

Beatrice laughed. "Oh, more than you can imagine. Don't worry—I do most of it. But the townsfolk appreciate having members of the nobility sponsor the event, and of course, we wouldn't be able to put it on without the generous funding that your family provides."

"I'm sure," Caspian murmured, rubbing his thumb across the spine of a neatly bound book sitting on her desk.

"It's a great experience for the whole town, and it provides fellowship and a boost to our economy as we head into the winter," Beatrice continued.

"Well, I am glad to hear that you handle most of it," Caspian said. "Can you let me know what I'm expected to do?" He gave her a lazy grin. "My mother wasn't super forthcoming about the details of everything she usually does."

Beatrice opened the folder and began flipping through the pages within. "Of course. It's mostly little things, like approving plans and budget expenses. But it's also appreciated if you approach the vendors and the townsfolk about setting up their booths, or providing music, food, or lumber for the bonfire, or anything of that nature. They tend to take it better coming from a member of the nobility than they do from the town librarian when most of them won't even touch the library."

She gave a self-deprecating laugh and sighed as she went back to shuffling papers.

"Who started the library?" he asked. He'd missed all of it while he was in Riyel.

Beatrice smiled. "Lord Dunham. He wanted education to be freely accessible to the people in the town and he wanted them to be able to get knowledge of anything. I'm very appreciative of it, because I personally love reading, and getting paid to help the people in the town and the surrounding manors find everything they need to know is a privilege. But since many of the townsfolk don't utilize the library to the full extent they could, it also frees me up to do things like plan the Fall Festival with your mother. Or you, as the case may be." She pulled a piece of paper from the stack with a triumphant grin and held it out to him. "I knew this was in there somewhere."

Caspian took the piece of paper and set it down on the desk to examine it closer. It was a simple sketch of the town square, with booths outlined and jotted notes about who would be placed where.

"This is my proposed map of the festival," she said proudly. "It takes into account which vendors like and dislike each other, places all the food in one corner, and provides ample room for a bonfire, with sufficient space to keep children away from it, if all goes according to plan."

Caspian looked at the very thorough map. "And you just need me to approve this?"

"That's correct," Beatrice said with a smile. "Then, if you don't mind, it's helpful if you can take the map to all the vendors listed, ask if they would like a booth at the festival, and encourage them to do so, including the use of festival funds for whatever is necessary. Did your mother discuss the budget with you at all?"

He shook his head. "She only said that you knew what the budget was, and I had free rein to take more if necessary to have the best festival possible."

"Lady Rendon is wonderful," Beatrice said with a smile. "This festival wouldn't be what it is without her support. She also understands that sometimes some of the townsfolk need to be convinced to put in the extra work to close up their shops for the day and move out into the town square."

"What you're saying is that my mother bribes them?" Caspian asked.

"Monetary compensation may be involved," Beatrice said solemnly, but there was a twinkle in her eye.

"Between you and me, I think she's trying to bribe me to stay in town, too," Caspian said with a grin. "I think she wants to see me married and settled down, but I don't know that I'm ready for that yet."

Why had he just blurted that out?

Beatrice nodded. "Your mother does have a matchmaker's heart. I can tell. We are kindred spirits in that sense."

Caspian sighed. "Yes, well, she has a challenge on her hands with me."

Was it true that he wasn't ready, though? Did he want to settle down?

The thought of Sophia sitting next to another man in the café made him uneasy, which was a new feeling for him. Maybe Sophia didn't like the man. Maybe she would be happy for Caspian to swoop in and save the day. Or maybe she was in love with the other man, and he'd misread their conversation in the goat pen.

He was getting way ahead of himself. He grunted and crossed his arms.

Focus, Caspian.

"Is there anything else you need from me today?" he asked as he uncrossed his arms. "How quickly do you need me to get to all of these vendors?"

"If you can speak to them all within the next week, that would be lovely," Beatrice said, "so we can continue planning. And yes, that is all I need today. Thank you so much for coming, and I hope we can make this the best Fall Festival we've ever had."

"I look forward to it," Caspian said, offering his hand. Beatrice held out hers and he took it, bowing slightly before letting go. They walked out of her office to find two old ladies in the library.

"Beatrice," one of them said, "where have you been?"

"Hello, Eugenia," Beatrice responded. "I was just in my office. How can I help you?"

"I'm looking for a new crocheting pattern," Eugenia responded, "but who's this handsome man?"

He'd grown a beard since he'd left, but surely Eugenia hadn't forgotten him entirely. She'd been the local schoolteacher, and even though he and his brothers had been taught by a tutor in their home, she'd still known them through town events. Perhaps she was only teasing?

"It's Lord Caspian Rendon," Beatrice said, giving Eugenia a stern glance.

"Oh. goodness, Lord Caspian," Eugenia said. "I had forgotten how handsome you were. Make sure you save a dance for me at the Fall Festival, won't you, dear?"

"Of course I will," Caspian said, after a quick glance at Beatrice. She was shaking her head, but Caspian didn't see a way out of this one without being impossibly rude, and he had a feeling that would make his mother terribly cranky.

"How many hearts did you break while you were gone?" Eugenia asked.

Caspian bit back a sigh. He hadn't missed the gossipy old ladies while he was in Riyel. They were lovely women, but they sure did know how to talk. No doubt word of his return would be everywhere shortly. "No broken hearts," he said. "Now if you'll excuse me, I have to head for home. Beatrice, ladies," he said, nodding in farewell as he walked out the door.

Even the brisk breeze and the sunshine did nothing to lift his mood as he made his way toward the café.

He'd thought that the Fall Festival was the first sign that his parents trusted him and wanted him to take care of something. But not only was he taking over his mother's least important task, it seemed to require dealing with the town gossips—not exactly something he wanted to be doing.

Caspian sighed as he entered the café. Being home wasn't going the way he'd expected at all.

He scanned the room for Sophia, but she wasn't there. She must have already left for home. He sighed again and made his way to the counter to order a hot cider. At least he could get a good drink out of this whole disappointing afternoon.

Besides, it was probably better if he didn't spend time with Sophia.

It would be a little too easy to fall for her.

Chapter Five
Sophia

Sophia tied the end of the rope lead around Ivy's neck as she prepared to open the gate. Valley and Meadow stayed with her pretty well, and of course the kids followed their mothers, but Ivy...she liked to run away as often as she possibly could.

There was a reason Sophia rarely opened the gate.

But she was taking them to a new pen today at the stable master's request. He'd said the northern pens were full of weeds, and asked if she could take them there. The goats would be thrilled—as long as she could get them there safely without losing any of them.

She held the rope tight and eased the gate open, bracing herself for Ivy to lunge forward like she always did. The kids ran out first, followed by Valley and Meadow at a stately pace, with Ivy doing her best to drag Sophia down the barn hallway.

"Would you calm down?" Sophia said to the goat, pulling back with all her might. "We'll get there just as fast if you stop fighting me so much."

Ivy didn't listen. She never did.

But at least it made Sophia feel better to admonish her as they made their way out the barn toward the pen.

She was halfway through the courtyard when she noticed Liliana approaching, with Caspian following behind her. Sophia smiled at the two of them. Caspian must have earned the task of following Liliana today.

Liliana burst into a run to catch up to her.

"Sophia, Sophia," she exclaimed, "where are you taking the goats today?"

"We're going to the pasture to the north," Sophia said.

"Can I help?" Liliana asked, reaching out to take the lead rope.

Sophia shook her head. "I'm not going to let go. But if you want to help hold the rope, you can."

Liliana grabbed onto the rope and hummed a happy little song as she started skipping next to Ivy. If she'd had a lead rope on Valley or Meadow, Liliana could have held them on her own, but Ivy was mischievous.

Sophia looked over to Caspian as he caught up to them. He smiled at her, and her stomach turned into butterflies. Somehow, he seemed more handsome every time she saw him.

"Out for a walk?" he asked.

Sophia shook her head. "The stable master asked me to take them to one of the pastures to help clear it out."

"I see this one requires a little extra attention." He glanced at the rope around Ivy's neck, which Liliana had already let go of.

Sophia laughed. "Yes, Ivy is a special one. The others like to stay with me. Her, not so much."

"Would you like some help?" Caspian asked, extending a hand, and Sophia gratefully relinquished control of the rope.

Realizing that the rope had changed hands, Ivy attempted to burst into a run again, but Caspian held tight.

After a moment, Ivy realized it was useless. He had a much firmer hand than Sophia, and probably weighed more than Ivy, something Sophia wasn't sure she could claim.

Ivy was not only the oldest goat, but she was also the largest by far, and sometimes she was a little more than Sophia could manage—not that she'd admit that to anyone. She didn't need anyone else taking her job.

"Thank you for your help," Sophia said as they passed through the gate and she avoided tripping over Mollie, who was trying to weave in and out underneath her dress.

"Of course," he said. "Liliana wanted to introduce me to her goats anyway."

"She does love the goats," Sophia said.

A few feet in front of them, Liliana looked back with a mischievous grin. "I love them, I love them, I love them," she sang in a high voice.

"She's also started making up songs about them," Sophia said knowingly as Liliana continued to sing some nonsense words.

"I see," Caspian said with a grimace as Liliana's voice reached never-before-heard notes.

"The goats love it," Sophia said as Mollie ran up to Liliana.

"I'm glad someone does," Caspian said diplomatically, looking down at Sophia with a grin.

They quickly reached the fence for the northern pasture and Sophia led the way to the gate. "I want to go in with the goats," Liliana announced.

"Of course," Caspian said.

Sophia reached for the gate, not realizing that Caspian was as well. Their hands touched and Sophia could almost swear that a spark passed between their hands before they both pulled away and looked at each other.

The butterflies that had faded were back in full force and she couldn't look away from his dark brown eyes. She took a step forward before she realized what she was doing, then took a step back.

But even with the distance between them, he was still looking deep into her eyes, and she couldn't remember what she'd been doing until Liliana said, "Can I open the gate?"

The spell broke and they looked away from each other, turning to look at Liliana.

"Let me get the gate for you," Sophia said, shaking herself as she reached over to open the gate.

Liliana ran in and the goats followed her, including Ivy as Caspian let go of the rope. Caspian latched the gate behind the goats and the girl and Sophia couldn't help smiling at the sight of the golden-haired girl running in the sunshine, the four baby goats chasing her. The mothers immediately set to eating the weeds that had sprung up since the last time they'd been to the north pasture.

She leaned against the fence, her arms resting on one of the lower boards. She loved days like today, when the sun was shining, the cool breeze of fall was stirring up the air, and the goats were happily eating weeds. The manor also had a few cows, but they didn't like the weeds the way the goats did, so there was always plenty for them to eat when they went around to the different pastures.

"I have a question for you," Caspian said, turning to look down at her.

"Oh?" Sophia didn't want to look at him, afraid that if she did, she would get dizzy with the closeness of him. She was incredibly aware of how near he was, so close she could probably brush against him without moving more than an inch.

Why was he so close?

"Will you help me with the Fall Festival?"

Of all the questions he could have asked, that was not one she would have expected, or could have ever guessed.

What did helping him with the Fall Festival entail? Would she even be capable of helping with it?

"I don't know anything about it," she admitted.

"My mother is in charge of hosting the Fall Festival in the town every year. This year, she wants me to get involved. And I'll be honest, I feel like I'm in over my head, given that I've never had anything to do with the Fall Festival except attending it and enjoying myself. I was hoping you would be willing to help me."

Sophia still couldn't look up at him. She would start blushing if she did. Why did he want her help? Was it because he'd felt the spark between them when their hands had touched? Did he want to spend more time with her? Was he using this as an excuse?

"I don't know how much help I could be," she said slowly. "I'm new to town and I don't know anyone or anything about the Fall Festival. And I don't get very much time off since the goats always need someone to look after them. But if there's something I can help with, I'll be glad to do it."

And not just because she wanted to spend time with him, either.

She dared to glance up at him, though he didn't notice, his gaze focused on the activity within the pasture. "I noticed you were sitting with a bunch of people at the café when I walked past the other day," he said. "I'm assuming that they might be able to help with the festival."

"So you're just using me for my connections?" she teased.

He looked down at her with a grin. "Absolutely," he said with no trace of hesitation. "I figure I could use all the help I can get."

Sophia nodded gravely. "I agree. You need lots of help."

"What is that supposed to mean?" he asked, turning to face her, crossing his arms across his chest as he leaned against the fence with his shoulder.

"You don't even want to walk in the barn, and yet you're supposed to put on a Fall Festival. Won't that require getting dirty?"

He rolled his eyes at her. "I'll have you know I am perfectly used to walking in the barn. I just like it when the aisle is swept first."

Sophia laughed and climbed the fence to sit on top of the fence post. She loved sitting on the fence, twice as tall as her normal height, and looking out across Lord Rendon's land. "And I suppose you think that the aisle should be swept regularly?" she said, looking down at him.

"Of course," he said. "It's just proper barn maintenance."

Sophia smiled as he also climbed the fence and perched on the next post over, looking a little wobbly as he did his best to find a comfortable position.

Sitting on the fence was fun, but it wasn't extremely comfortable.

"I'll see what I can do about the festival," she said, "but you'll have to give me more specific details than just that you want access to my friends."

"Tell me more about your friends," he said. "Do they work in businesses in town?"

Sophia smiled as she thought about her friends.

The fact that she actually had friends was strange enough. For her to know them as well as she did after so short a time here felt incredibly strange. "Yes, they all work in different businesses around the town. It's so much fun to see the different things they're doing—they're all wonderful."

"Are any of them closer to you than others?" he asked, and something in his tone felt different. This felt more personal than the Fall Festival.

Sophia shook her head. "I know Thea the best because I see her every time I'm in town. The others tend to come in and out depending on who's working that day and who's free to stop by and say hello. But they all accept me for who I am, and don't mind that I'm new to town. I'm very thankful for them and their friendship."

Caspian looked as if he wanted to say something else, but he didn't, and Sophia didn't push.

"You should come to the café with me," she said. "I'm sure Thea and Dietrich and the others would be more than happy to get to know you."

"I might take you up on that offer." He stared at Liliana, who had given up on chasing the goats and was lying in the field while the goats climbed on top of her and chewed her hair. "I don't suppose Liliana has ever thought to protect her hair from the goats," he said, abruptly changing the topic.

Sophia shook her head. "No, she seems to enjoy the fact that goat spit turns her hair into sticks. She must take a bath far more regularly than I do."

Caspian shuddered. "I don't even want to think about my hair turning into a stick."

"Given that you don't have long hair, it's not an issue," Sophia said, the corners of her mouth turning up. "Although you could grow yours out just to experience it."

He shuddered again, nearly falling off his fence post.

"I don't suppose you want to try it," she continued teasing him. "After all, it does take forever to wash out. And if you don't get a regular bath, you might have your hair stuck together with goat spittle for a few days."

"Please stop." He shook his head rapidly. "I absolutely will not be doing that."

"Then it shouldn't bother you. If you're never going to grow your hair out to enjoy the experience of a baby goat sucking on it, you don't have to worry about it." She couldn't help the laugh that escaped as Caspian shuddered a third time and jumped off the fence post outside of the pasture.

"I will do nothing of the sort," he said, "and you know it."

Sophia laughed until her sides ached, with Caspian on the ground staring up at her, shaking his head in disbelief. "You're just having fun torturing me," he said, rolling his eyes.

"So what if I am?" she asked. "You're making it easy."

Caspian stared at her a moment, his expression unreadable, before making his way over to her and holding up both hands. "May I help you down?"

Sophia stared at his hands for a moment. Would she feel the same spark if she touched him again? There was no reason to turn him down, so she nodded, unable to find the words to say yes.

He put his hands on her waist and her heart beat faster as a spark flowed through her. He gently lifted her from the fence post, his eyes meeting hers the entire way as he lowered her to the ground. He paused a moment before letting go, his hands warm even through the fabric between them.

She'd never felt anything like this before.

The distance between them grew as he took a step back and she took a deep breath, not sure how things had changed between them and yet so sure that they had.

Whatever this was, surely he was feeling it, too. It couldn't be something that only she felt, this feeling that everything was changing.

Did he feel the same way?

Did he want something to happen between them?

Maybe someday, it would.

Maybe someday, he would become the family she'd always ached for.

Liliana rushed toward them, baby goats chasing her, and Sophia forced her attention back to her charges. Shame on her for getting distracted while she had the young lady with her.

But she couldn't regret the moment they'd shared, even if she should have been paying more attention to Liliana and the goats.

After they brought the goats back to the manor a few hours later, Caspian took Liliana back to the house and Sophia brought the goats back to their pen. When she exited the barn, she found Caspian leaning against the wall of the barn waiting for her.

"What are you up to?" she asked, raising an eyebrow at him.

"I don't suppose you want to go to town with me," he said with an easy grin.

Sophia narrowed her eyes. "Already? Why are you in such a rush?"

Was he just trying to get her alone?

He shrugged. "The Fall Festival is supposed to happen in a couple of weeks and apparently I'm really far behind on everything."

Sophia considered it. She had planned on mending her dress this evening, but it was beautiful weather, and a walk sounded lovely. Besides, it would give her an excuse to stop in and see Thea and maybe eat a meal in friendly company instead of in the manor kitchen with the staff, who still weren't sure what to make of her.

It was probably her fault that the rest of the manor staff weren't her friends. She hadn't been the friendliest when she'd arrived, preferring to keep her walls up and stay away from attention in her new home.

Maybe that was why Caspian was such a breath of fresh air. Like her friends at the café, he actively seemed to seek her out and enjoy her company. Everyone else at the manor seemed content to let her fade into the background.

That may have been what she wanted when she first arrived, but it had been almost a year. Surely by now, she could stop hiding and waiting for someone to come after her.

She should stop being so suspicious. It was time to stop concealing herself, and mending her dress could wait. She nodded. "I would love to go to town with you."

Chapter Six
Caspian

Caspian strode forward, eager to get to town and talk to Beatrice. Having Sophia on board to help introduce him to the townspeople seemed like a good plan, but since he'd been a fool and put down the copy of the map that Beatrice had made for him, he didn't know where to start.

Getting a copy of the map would help.

"Have you ever walked with someone much shorter than you?" Sophia asked from behind him, her breath heaving.

Caspian glanced down at her and grimaced.

"I'm sorry," he said, immediately slowing his pace. "I've gotten used to walking quickly during my time in Riyel. I haven't had anyone to walk with me in so long."

Sophia smiled up at him. "I don't mind running when I mean to run. But running to keep pace with someone for the entire walk to town is a little more than I had anticipated this evening."

Caspian let out a self-deprecating chuckle. "I apologize. I should pay greater attention. Especially considering I'm the one who invited you to join me."

"You did," she said, keeping pace with him easily now as they crested a hill and the town came into view. "What is your plan this evening?"

"I want to stop at the library and see if Beatrice is still there. I'd like to take a look at the stall assignments again and get a copy of the map she created so I know which vendors she has in mind. I was trying to avoid the grannies and forgot to bring home my copy of the map last time."

"The grannies?" she asked, her nose wrinkling as she looked up at him.

"Oh, yes, have you not met them yet? Lovely ladies, if a bit keen to spread any bit of gossip they can."

Sophia grinned. "Ah, I know the type. And if Beatrice is not there?"

"Then I want to stop at the café to see who I can meet there and start asking them to be vendors at the festival."

"I know the manor usually has a booth," Sophia said, "because I was told to make enough soap to sell at the Fall Festival. But I have no idea what that means or how much soap I should make. Nobody else does, either, because they didn't have goats before I came along."

Caspian glanced down at her. "You brought the goats?"

She shook her head. "No, they bought the goats from someone else. But they didn't buy them until I was there asking for a job. They asked if I had experience with goats, and I said that I did not, but I was more than willing to learn. I would have done just about anything for a job at that point," she said with a humorless laugh. "I desperately needed work, so I was more than grateful for any job they were willing to give me."

Before Caspian could ask why she'd been so desperately in need of a job, she continued. "And honestly, I don't mind the goats. I didn't expect to love them as much as I do, but they bring me great comfort, and I have loved getting to know them and all the different ways they can manage to get out of a fence...even if it makes for some interesting evenings. It's always evening, you know. They never get out during the day. It's always when it's most inconvenient for me."

Caspian laughed. "I'm sure it is. I am glad there are goats at the manor, though. Liliana had been begging for them for years, ever since she saw some at the Fall Festival and fell in love with them. I'm honestly surprised it took so long for them to humor her."

"Maybe they were just waiting for the right person for the job to come along," Sophia said with a shrug. "Either way, I'm glad they're my responsibility."

Only a few moments later, they were walking through the front door of the library. Sophia looked around with a smile and saw Beatrice first, hurrying over to give her a hug.

"Hello," Beatrice said, giving Sophia a hug. "I wasn't expecting to see you this evening. Is everything alright?"

"Caspian asked if I could come with him and help with the festival for a little bit," Sophia said.

Beatrice gave Sophia a knowing look and Caspian took a deep breath.

He knew what that look meant.

It meant something to do with him.

What exactly, he wasn't sure, but he would bet money that it was Beatrice trying to figure out what was going on between him and Sophia.

He wanted to know, too, because he had a feeling he was heading for trouble.

"Do you still have that copy of the map for me?" he asked before anyone could exchange any more glances. "I forgot to bring it home last time. And do you know if the manor's booth is large enough for them to add Sophia's soap in addition to everything else they usually do?"

"We can't forget my soaps," Sophia said cheerily.

"Of course I won't forget your soaps! You know I love them," Beatrice said.

"I've never tried them before," Caspian said.

Beatrice narrowed her eyes. "You haven't?"

Actually, it was probably the soap that was in his bath. "Maybe I have, if it's the soap they use on the estate."

"That's probably it," Sophia said with a smile.

"It's great soap," he said.

How had his life changed from training to be a guard in the city to discussing how lovely a bar of soap was with a beautiful woman in his small town's library?

"Let's go take a look," Beatrice said, and Caspian and Sophia followed her into her office. As he waited for her to pull out the file with the map, he watched Sophia take in the cozy but crowded office. Her hand reached out and caressed the spine of a leather-bound book as Beatrice dropped the file on her desk.

"I was thinking the manor could be here," Beatrice said, pointing to a large square on the hand-sketched map of town. "But again, it all depends on which other vendors you can get to be a part of the festival."

Caspian nodded, leaning over to get a closer look. "I think that's a good spot for it. Most people will walk past it on their way to get food."

"As long as you can get food vendors," Beatrice said in a sprightly tone. "I don't suppose you've had any progress in that quarter."

He shook his head. "Not yet."

Caspian reached for a pencil at the same time as Sophia did, and their hands accidentally touched. He felt a jolt of energy run through him for the second time that day.

Sophia was different from any other girl he'd known.

He'd accidentally—and not so accidentally—brushed hands with more than a few girls in his lifetime, and he'd never felt like this before.

This was uncharted territory for him.

As a thirdborn son, he was supposed to marry a noble girl with a large dowry.

Knowing that hadn't kept him from flirting with girls over the years. He'd always managed to flirt without falling in love.

His parents had married for love, somehow finding each other within their circle of nobility. He'd always wanted that for himself...but his circle of eligible girls wasn't very large, and it certainly didn't include Sophia.

Life would look very different than he'd planned if he married a milk-maid.

He wasn't sure he was prepared for that, even as he wondered what a life with Sophia could be like.

He brushed off the thought and reached for the pencil again.

This had to stop. He didn't want to lead her on. If there was no chance of a future for the two of them, he shouldn't be spending time with her.

And yet, he didn't want to stop spending time with her.

"I think that will work," he said, making a small x in the corner of the square that Beatrice had suggested for the manor's booth. "Perhaps we'll start tonight at the café."

Sophia perked up at the idea of going to the café, as he'd known she would.

"I was on my way there shortly," Beatrice said. "I plan to enjoy Thea's dinner since I don't want to cook for myself tonight." She laughed. "My father is off in Riyel, and I don't feel like putting in the effort if it's just me."

"Understandable," Sophia said with a smile, grabbing her friend's hand. "Let's go see what deliciousness Thea has cooked up." She paused, and turned to Caspian, her smile falling. "Actually, I need to go home. I didn't plan on going to town today and forgot my purse."

"I'll pay for your dinner," Caspian said. "I'm the one who changed your plans for the evening. It would be wrong of me to invite you out and not feed you."

Beatrice smirked at Sophia again and Caspian's stomach felt off. This was definitely leading her on, but what was he supposed to do? Leave her hungry?

"It's not as if Thea would turn you away," Beatrice said, nudging Sophia's shoulder with her own. "Even if you weren't good for it later."

They made their way to the Cozy Cat Café, and it wasn't long before Caspian found himself in the middle of a large group of people, most of whom looked familiar but none that he could name except Thea.

He'd grown up here, and yet, he barely knew anyone in town.

He should change that if he stayed in the Northlands.

Thea was serving up a large pot pie which smelled absolutely amazing, and everyone around the table was diving in.

Caspian held out his plate for a serving of the pot pie. He could feel curious stares from everyone around the table. Should he introduce himself? Wait for Sophia, Thea, or Beatrice to do it? He felt completely out of his depth in this scenario.

"Everyone, this is Caspian," Sophia said after a moment, and he smiled down at her before making eye contact with everyone around the large table. "He's helping Beatrice plan the Fall Festival."

"How go the preparations?" Thea asked from her place at the head of the table.

"They're going well," Caspian said. "I was actually going to ask if you would be willing to serve food there, either as a booth, or having the café open. A booth would be preferable, but I'll take anything I can get," he said with a grin. "Everyone says your food is the best."

Thea smiled slightly and nodded. "I was planning on it. I don't suppose you know where my booth would be?"

"Right next to the café, if that's where you want to be," Beatrice piped up.

"Then count me in," she said. "Does anyone else at this table want to sign up as well?"

Across from him, a man nodded. "I'll help you, Thea," he said. "You'll need a second person."

Caspian fought the urge to squint at him.

He was the man that Sophia had been sitting with.

"Definitely," Thea said with a smile. "Thank you for the help."

He was older than he'd looked from a distance. Maybe ten or fifteen years older than Sophia appeared, though his hair flopped over his forehead in the style of a much younger man.

And Sophia had barely looked at him since they'd arrived.

Maybe there wasn't anything between them.

"The blacksmith will have a booth," the young lady with dark hair sitting next to Thea said. "Mark us down."

"And I can probably get the tailor to have a booth as well," the young man next to her said.

Beatrice clapped her hands. "This is wonderful. Thank you, everyone. I'm hopeful that this year will be the best yet—and of course, if anyone wants to donate wood for the bonfire, please let me know."

"I'll see what I can do," yet another young man said across the table.

There was silence then, as everyone turned their attention to eating Thea's pot pie as quickly as possible. It was absolutely delicious. "I think Cook needs to learn a thing or two about pot pie from Thea," Caspian said to Sophia.

"Her pot pies are lacking, it is true," Sophia said with a grin.

"She's a fantastic cook in everything else," Caspian said. "But this is phenomenal."

Thea stood, the legs of her chair scraping against the floor. "May I have a word with you?" she asked Caspian.

He swallowed a sigh as he stood and followed her across the room. He should have known this was coming.

"Lord Caspian," Thea began once they were far enough away that they wouldn't be heard.

"Call me Caspian, please," he said.

"I'm going to be honest with you, Caspian," the older woman said. "I see the way you're looking at Sophia. Do you have the intention of wooing her or is she simply something for you to enjoy while you're here for a short while? Because she deserves better than for you to have fun with her and then leave for Riyel again."

Caspian didn't have an answer to the question. He'd been wrestling with it all evening and hadn't come any closer to figuring it out. "I'll let you know when I have an answer to that," he said after a moment.

Thea shook her head. "You're going to break her heart. You should know that we won't willingly stand by and watch you hurt her."

Caspian glanced at the table, where the man who'd been with Sophia was staring at him. "Is there something there?" he asked.

Thea followed his gaze and smiled when she saw who was looking at them. She shook her head. "No, there is nothing between them, but Dietrich is very protective of Sophia. He was the one who found her outside of town and brought her to me. They're good friends, and nothing more. Not that it should matter to you. I should hope you would realize how much she has to lose, and how little you do. I don't want to see her get hurt."

Thea was right. It wasn't right for him to lead her on while he was still trying to figure out what he was doing himself.

He should stop spending time with Sophia, leave her alone, let her get back to her life.

He didn't want to hurt her.

"I hear you," he said gravely. "I will leave her alone."

Thea nodded, the worry lines between her eyes easing as she looked over at the table where Sophia was laughing at Beatrice. "I hoped you would understand," she said. "The only thing she has going for her is her determination not to let life bring her down, and I would hate to see anything diminish her fire. I couldn't stand by and watch without saying something."

Caspian made a noise in the back of his throat that felt something like agreement, but also irritation at the meddlesome ways of the townspeople. He wasn't going to hurt Sophia. On purpose, at least.

It shouldn't bother him that Sophia had people who cared for her enough to stand up to Lord Rendon's son on her behalf. But it bothered him a little that they thought badly enough of him to think she needed their interference.

Caspian followed Thea back to the table and sat down in his seat next to Sophia, who glanced up at him curiously. He shook his head and turned his attention back to his pot pie.

Thea was right. Sophia deserved better than someone who might not be here in two months. And right now, she wouldn't get that from him.

He needed to leave her alone.

Chapter Seven

Sophia

Sophia and Caspian began the walk home in comfortable silence, though the comfort soon faded. Sophia wasn't sure what had changed, but Caspian was more withdrawn than usual.

He hadn't been the same since Thea had pulled him aside in the café. What had she said to him to put him in this mood?

"Thank you for dinner," she said after a moment of silence that lasted far too long. "It was delicious."

"Yes, it was," Caspian said shortly. "I'll have to ask for her recipe and see if Cook can make it for us."

Sophia laughed. "I don't know if she'll give it to you."

Caspian shoved his hands into his pockets and gave her half a smile. "If I was her, I wouldn't give out that recipe. Maybe if you asked for it—she likes you better than me, I'm sure."

That seemed like an understatement. "She didn't seem very happy to see you, did she?" Sophia asked.

Neither had Dietrich. She would have to ask them why they didn't like Caspian the next time she was there. He had been a perfect gentleman so far, and she saw no reason not to like him. But maybe they knew something she didn't know. She was new to town, after all. Maybe there was more to the story.

Maybe that's why everyone was so surprised to see him, why Thea had pulled him aside to talk to him and why Dietrich was glaring at him.

It would do her no good to get involved with a scoundrel.

It was hard to tell much about him from the limited time they'd spent together, and she knew nothing except that he had been a guard in Riyel for two years.

It was time to change that. If she learned more about him, maybe she could discover why nobody seemed to like seeing them together.

Nobody except Beatrice, who had done nothing but smirk at her the entire night. Beatrice seemed to think that they made a cute couple, like one of her romance books, but romance books didn't happen in real life.

And Beatrice might be disappointed, especially since there seemed to be some reason for Thea and Dietrich to dislike him. She trusted their opinion—because if she couldn't trust Thea and Dietrich, who else could she trust?

Probably not Caspian.

The thought made her feel something. What feeling exactly, she wasn't sure. It wasn't sadness. It wasn't hurt. Maybe uncomfortable...but it went deeper than that.

Whatever the feeling was, she wanted to trust Caspian.

She would have to do something to determine whether he was worthy of her trust, starting with talking to Thea and Dietrich.

"I suppose we should probably pretend we didn't eat in town and still go to dinner," she said, looking up at him. He hadn't answered her question.

"I think we may have to," he agreed. "I don't know how much I'll be able to eat after Thea's pot pie, though."

"It was so filling," Sophia said. But if she didn't make an appearance at dinner, someone would notice.

Probably.

Maybe not.

She didn't want to find out, though. It was easier to avoid being noticed.

As they approached the manor and made their way through the gates, Sophia glanced up at him one more time.

Perhaps Beatrice was onto something. He certainly was handsome.

But if she couldn't trust him, it didn't matter how handsome he was.

"I'll see you later," she said as she split off toward the maids' quarters.

Caspian nodded toward her and headed for the front of the manor house. He waved as he strode away and Sophia waved back, before hurrying to freshen up for dinner.

When she arrived in the dining room used by the servants and guards, Caspian wasn't there.

She ate her dinner in silence, surrounded by housemaids who didn't want to talk to her because she worked in the barn, stable hands who joked amongst themselves but ignored her because she was a woman, and kitchen staff who were perfectly polite when she worked among them but never really included her.

She hadn't realized how nice it was to feel included until Caspian.

Where had he gone? Was he avoiding her?

Had she turned someone else away from being her friend?

She'd always spent a fair amount of time alone, whether she was at Lady Manning's in Riyel or here in the Northlands. Rosaleen was the only person who'd ever loved her.

Was there something wrong with her? Was she that difficult to work with? Did she make people uncomfortable? She'd thought that leaving Lady Manning behind would change that, but even now, she was still surrounded by strangers.

Loneliness stabbed through her as she ate a few more bites of mashed potatoes and smushed the rest around her plate to look like she'd eaten more than she had.

Maybe she was just broken.

But her friends at the café didn't seem to think she was broken. Or if they did, they did a really good job of hiding it. Maybe she wasn't broken.

Maybe it was just the people at the manor...and at Lady Manning's...and now Caspian was also avoiding her.

The evidence seemed to be piling up to suggest she wasn't someone worthy of love.

Sophia sighed and brought her plate to the kitchen, scraped it off, and washed it before heading back to the room she shared with the housemaids. She sat down on her bed and began to unlace her boots before realization slammed into her.

The goats.

She hadn't checked on them since she left for town with Caspian.

She sighed and relaced her boots. At least her goats loved her.

She made her way out to the goat pen and Mollie immediately ran to her. Sophia crouched on the ground and pulled Mollie into her arms, picking her up and scratching under her chin. "I'm so glad I have you," she whispered to the baby goat, squishing her in a tight hug. "You make everything better."

Mollie accepted the hug for a moment, but then began to wiggle while simultaneously trying to eat Sophia's hair. "Now, now," Sophia said. "I don't need my hair to be all sticky until my next bath."

She'd forgotten to tie it up before coming in, which was her own mistake, and she immediately put Mollie down so she could rectify that. She pulled a strip of fabric from her dress pocket and tied back her long hair.

"I don't suppose you want to talk to me," she said to Mollie, rubbing the top of her head. "Apparently nobody else here does. I'm sure Liliana would talk to me if I asked, but for some reason, I think she might be the only one who would. As much as I love listening to Liliana tell her stories and talk to you, I would prefer to talk to some adults. But since none of them seem to be interested, I'll have to settle for you," she said to the baby goat, leaning over to rub her nose against Mollie's.

Mollie pushed against her face before pulling back and attempting to head-butt her. Sophia had no interest in attempting a head-butting competition with a goat, whose skull seemed to be much harder than hers, and pulled back as the other goats swarmed around them, attracted to her leaning down.

The adults nosed around her pockets, hoping that she'd brought food with her. "I'm sorry, I didn't bring anything," she told the goats. "I should have known better than to get your hopes up, but really, I had to come check on you. If you wouldn't knock over your water all the time, I'd check on you less and you wouldn't get your hopes up nearly as often. I'll go get you something before I go to bed. Or maybe I'll be mean and make you wait until breakfast. You shouldn't be eating so much anyway."

The goats grumbled but gave up when they realized she didn't have food and went back to browsing outside while the baby goats tried to climb all over Sophia.

"I don't suppose any of you want to tell me that you love me and you think I'm amazing," she asked the goats with a wry smile. "No? I didn't think so."

At least she knew, whether they said it or not, that they loved her.

It would have been nice to hear somebody say it, though.

There was a lump in her throat and her eyes hurt as she thought about the fact that she was twenty-something years old and she didn't have anyone to love her.

She didn't even know how old she was exactly—there had never been anyone in her life who cared to remember that fact or tell her about it. Lady Manning had taken even the dignity of having a birthday from her.

Sophia sighed. It was easy to blame Lady Manning, even if it wasn't necessarily true—it was less painful if it wasn't her fault or the fault of the parents she'd never known.

When she was younger, she'd dreamed of her parents returning from some far-flung place and rescuing her.

She didn't dream of that anymore.

"Goodnight, babies," Sophia said, catching Mollie around the neck and pulling her closer so she could kiss the top of her head. "Sleep well."

She made her way outside and climbed the fence west of the barn, perching on a fence post and looking up at the stars. The crisp fall air felt wonderful, though she wished she'd grabbed her cloak before leaving her room. She wrapped her arms around herself and took a deep breath, closing her eyes and just breathing for a moment.

It would have been nice if her life had been different, but she couldn't change it now. She could only move forward with the life that she already had. If that meant she was going to spend the rest of her life looking for someone to love her, she would do that.

It couldn't be possible for someone to spend their whole life without finding anyone who would love them, right?

She had to believe it wasn't possible.

There was a noise as a door somewhere opened and shut, and Sophia looked over to see Caspian wandering toward her.

Relief poured through her. He wasn't avoiding her—or he was doing a very bad job of it if he was.

He paused a few feet away from her and gave her a look she couldn't figure out. "I thought you were avoiding me," she said simply.

Caspian sighed and climbed the fence next to her. "I probably should," he said, "but I can't seem to stay away, even if I wanted to."

"What does that mean?" she asked softly.

"Thea doesn't want me to hurt you," he said, his shoulder brushing against hers. He didn't look at her, staring up at the stars instead. "I don't want to hurt you. I don't know what my future looks like here, and I don't want to lead you on."

"You're not going to hurt me," she said.

"You just told me that you thought I was avoiding you. That feels like hurting you."

Sophia ignored the sharpness that stabbed her gut at the reminder. "I don't mind."

He let out a humorless chuckle. "I don't think Dietrich and Thea feel the same way."

"Did Dietrich say something, too?" she asked.

He shook his head. "Not yet. But it's not just them. I don't want to hurt you, either. I just don't know what I'm doing." He sighed, shifting on the fence, getting a little closer to her. "I used to look up at the stars when I was training in the city. They're so much brighter here, but it still comforted me to know that I was looking at the same stars that they were looking at back home."

"I find it hard to believe how much brighter they are here," Sophia said. It still amazed her to look at them.

"Have you been to the city?" Caspian asked, looking down at her.

"I lived and worked in Riyel from when I was a wee thing until this spring," Sophia said, shrugging her shoulders, the motion causing her to brush against him. "I never left the city before I came here." She shivered at the memory of her journey when she'd fled, and how Dietrich had saved her. He'd brought her to Thea, who'd fed her, clothed her, and found her a job with Lord Rendon.

Without Dietrich and Thea, she wouldn't have made it.

"I had to leave, or I would still be there now," she said absentmindedly.

"Why did you have to leave?" Caspian asked, pulling off his coat and dropping it over her shoulders.

It was warm, and it smelled like him.

It was wonderful.

Sophia chewed on her bottom lip. She hadn't meant to get into her past—how could she say it without him thinking she was overreacting or thinking it was worse than it was? "I thought I might be in danger if I stayed," she said finally. "So I left."

Caspian frowned at her. "What do you mean, in danger?" he asked. "Are you still in danger?"

Sophia shivered and looked up at the stars, avoiding eye contact. "I don't know," she admitted. "I would like to think that I'm not, but for all I know, she could still be looking for me."

"Is there danger to anyone else here?" Caspian asked quietly.

She took a deep breath. She hadn't even considered that her being here might bring trouble to Lord Rendon and his family. "I don't think so," she said after a moment. "Lady Manning would have nothing to gain from harming anyone here. It's me she hated. Rosaleen told me I couldn't come back for her, or even send word, because she didn't want Lady Manning to be able to find me. So I don't know if she's still looking for me, but even if she was, everyone else should be safe."

Caspian wrapped his arm around her, and she leaned into his warmth. "I won't let her hurt you," he said, the strength in his voice reassuring. "I'll make sure you're safe. After all, it's my job."

They sat in silence, looking up at the stars, and Sophia felt a peace she'd never felt before. Maybe he did care. Maybe she wasn't entirely unlovable. Sure, it was his job, but there had to be more to it than that.

None of the other guards had ever put their arm around her while they looked up at the stars.

That had to count for something.

Chapter Eight
CASPIAN

CASPIAN WAS ALMOST OUT the front door, almost to freedom, when his mother's voice called him from down the hallway. "Caspian, would you come to the study, please?"

Could he pretend he hadn't heard her, or pretend that it wasn't him?

No. She would know, and he knew better than to ignore his mother. So he turned and made his way to the study, where both his parents were waiting for him.

His mother sat in her favorite chair in his father's study. It was a cozy chair that he knew for a fact was only there because his father enjoyed it when his mother sat with him while he worked. Lord Rendon sat behind his desk, his hands folded across his stomach as he leaned back in his chair. The pose should have meant he was relaxed, but Caspian could see the tension in his eyes.

Oh, lovely. Apparently, they were about to have a fun conversation.

"We're so glad you're home," his mother began.

Caspian sighed. There was a "but" coming.

"But you haven't spent any time with us, and I miss you," Lady Rendon continued. "Come chat with us. What have you been up to since you got back?"

Caspian shrugged. "I've been eating dinner with you."

"And that's the only reason you came home?" Lord Rendon asked sternly. "To eat dinner with us?"

Lady Rendon shook her head at his father. "I know you don't have long before you have to make the decision about whether you're renewing your contract for the next year, and I have a feeling your future won't find you here in the Northlands. I would like to spend time with you before you leave us again to find your future in Riyel, whether it's in the Guard or in a hunt for a wife."

Caspian's eyes widened at the mention of marriage, and he started pacing the room rather than make eye contact with either of his parents. "It's not that I'm trying to avoid spending time with you," he said, "but I'm busy. I've been doing the festival like you asked me to, and training the guard and—"

"And that's lovely," his mother said. "I'm sure you're doing a wonderful job. Has Beatrice been helpful?"

"Yes, she has been. I think the festival is coming along well." He came to a halt in front of his mother. "Are you missing it?" he teased.

"Yes," she admitted, "but I'm enjoying the respite, and I'm sure I'll be back in the role next year."

He opened his mouth to protest that he might be around to continue it next year but closed it.

It wasn't likely, and they both knew it.

"I must say, I am looking forward to seeing what you do with the festival. You're growing up, my son. Soon your thoughts will turn to finding a wife, and I know what that entails. I know you'll look for a wealthy girl who has a good dowry and can help you buy your own estate—and since I prefer the country to being in Riyel, that means I most likely won't see you as much." His mother let out a tiny laugh. "I do love it here in the Northlands, you know. I love the festivals and the small town and the freedom to be ourselves and not be caught up in the chaos that surrounds the court."

"It was a wonderful way to grow up," Caspian admitted. "I'm glad that Liliana has more freedom than we did."

"As am I," Lady Rendon said, smiling at the portrait of their family that graced the wall to her right. "Speaking of your sister, she wishes to spend more time with you. Do you think you could start dining with us for luncheon, too?"

Caspian frowned, drumming his fingers against his father's desk. "I've been eating with the guards for lunch, trying to get to know them better."

"A good effort," his father said, finally speaking up. "Please continue to do so."

His mother sighed. "Just today, maybe? The rest of the time you can eat with the guards. And dear, will you please try to spend more time with Liliana and your brothers?"

Caspian nodded. He also missed spending time with his brothers. What he wouldn't give to go back to the days when they were young and carefree and played and roamed the entire Northlands.

But they were grown up now, and things had to change. Kellan was training to become their father's heir, he was a member of the Royal Guard, and Gideon...well, no one actually knew anything about what Gideon did. He seemed perfectly content to flit around and disappear whenever the mood struck him—though his supposed role was managing the books for the estate.

"I will spend more time with them," he promised. He gave his mother a kiss on the cheek, and she used the opportunity to pull him in for a hug.

"Thank you," she said softly. "That's all I wanted."

He let her hold him for a moment longer than he liked before disengaging and getting to his feet to leave the study. "I'll be back for lunch. Actually—"

His parents looked at him expectantly.

"Do you know Lord and Lady Manning?"

His mother sighed. "Such a sad story."

Oh, really?

His father cleared his throat. "Lord Manning was a good man. His first wife died not long after their daughter was born."

"She was a lovely thing, but not very strong," Lady Rendon said.

"And only a few months after Lord Manning remarried, both Lord Manning and his daughter passed away."

"Was it said why?" Caspian asked.

Lord Rendon shook his head. "No. It was a pity, though. Blanche was the sweetest little thing. You played with her once when Manning and I were in court."

"She was right around your age," his mother said softly. "I felt so horrible knowing she would grow up without a mother, though of course her father loved her very much. I wouldn't be surprised if heartbreak took him off if she went first."

Caspian nodded. "Thank you."

"Why do you ask?" his mother asked.

"Oh, a friend mentioned them, and I wondered if you knew them. I thought the name seemed familiar, but you know I don't know all the nobility like Kellan does."

"They lived just down the street from us in Riyel," his mother said, "but I was busy with you three and didn't get to know them well. I haven't thought about them since we moved here. Such a pity young Blanche passed, though. She would have been a good match for you if she hadn't."

Caspian fought the urge to roll his eyes as he turned to leave again. Always thinking about marriage. "Thank you both. I love you."

"Are you sure you don't want to talk about potential girls you could court?" his mother asked hopefully.

"Definitely not," Caspian said, escaping out the door.

"We love you, too," his mother called after him as he disappeared down the hallway.

He sighed as he made it to the front door. She was right. He needed to spend more time with his family. It wasn't like he was trying to avoid them. If anything, he wished he could spend more time with them.

He didn't appreciate being brought into his father's study and scolded, though.

Not to mention the way she'd talked about him getting married soon. Why wasn't she harping on Kellan and Gideon? They were older than him. They should be focused on getting married, not him. And yet, she was talking to him like the entire fate of the family lineage rested on him.

That wasn't really fair. But he didn't want to think about marriage yet. He was busy enough with the festival and training the guard.

Maybe he was spending a little more time than expected with a certain milkmaid.

But even if he wasn't spending time with her, he wouldn't have time to think about marriage yet.

He gritted his teeth as he made his way through the courtyard to the section that they used as a training arena. "Hopkins," he called to one of the guards walking through the courtyard. "Come duel me."

He wanted to hit something with a sword.

Hopkins would do.

This counted as training, right?

He made his way through several guards before his older brother appeared in front of him.

The idea of fighting his brother made pleasure surge through him. They'd sparred for hours as children, but it had been a while, and he'd learned a lot of skills since then.

He was ready to trounce his brother.

"Had enough yet?" Kellan asked, grinning as he gripped his sword and settled into his stance.

Truthfully, he'd been about to call it quits before his brother appeared, but now he wouldn't dream of it.

"Worried I'm going to beat you?" Caspian asked.

The guards that he'd already sparred began to circle around them, joined by several others.

"Never," Kellan said, pressing forward.

Their spar was fierce but short as Kellan withdrew after only a few minutes. "Wouldn't want you to hurt yourself," he said as he leaned forward to clasp Caspian's hand.

"I'm sure you're just trying to save face," Caspian teased, looking at the ring of guards that surrounded them.

He would have lost to make Kellan look good if necessary. Kellan needed the respect of the men here, and Caspian had fought enough of them and won to have solidified his standing as a good soldier.

"If that's what lets you sleep at night," Kellan said, passing off the sword to a guard. "I'll see you later?"

"Definitely," Caspian said with a smile.

It had been good to fight his brother again. This probably wasn't his mother's idea of spending time with his brother...and yet, they'd spent time together.

And now he was thinking about his mother's conversation again. So much for getting it out of his mind.

Caspian wiped the sweat off his brow and grumbled as he made his way to the kitchen. He'd worked up an appetite, and it was still an hour until lunch. Maybe he could find something to steal.

Or find a certain someone.

Anything to distract himself again now that his muscles were too worn out to provide physical distraction.

Caspian walked into the kitchen and found it full of bustling people and a nervous energy. He scanned the room, pretending that he wasn't looking for a certain girl amongst the crowd. But there, in the corner, was Sophia. She was wrapping a roll of butter, seemingly oblivious to the chaos around her.

He made his way over to her and plopped down on the tall stool that was conveniently in the corner near her.

"What's wrong with you?" she asked. "You look grumpier than Ivy when I forget to give her a treat with her afternoon feed."

"Family is complicated, and I hate it," Caspian said with a groan.

Sophia smiled softly to herself as she wrapped the butter and sat it in a small bowl. "I wish I had a family to be complicated with."

Caspian paused. He didn't know what to say to that, but it was obvious that he'd said the wrong thing. If he didn't have his family, he would give anything to have them, and Sophia clearly didn't have any or she wouldn't be here in his mother's kitchen, alone despite all the people around her. "Sorry," he said. "I just, well, I, you know, it—"

"I'm used to it," Sophia said, cutting him off. "I just wish I had a family sometimes. Or all the time. It must be nice having them so close you can see them all the time."

Caspian nodded around the lump in his throat. He couldn't even imagine not having his family.

"Would you like a cup of tea?" Sophia asked him. "It always makes me feel better when I'm having a rough day."

Tea didn't seem like it would make his day better, but he nodded. "I'll take a cup."

What could it hurt?

"And let me guess, you're hungry?" Sophia said.

"I'm always hungry," Caspian said with a grin.

Sophia smirked at him and glanced around the room. "Give me a moment," she said before she made her way over to the fire, where a hot kettle waited, and poured water into two mugs. She added loose tea leaves to mesh bags and placed them into the mugs.

She brought the mugs over and handed them to him before bustling away again, making her way through the kitchen and pulling a slice of sourdough bread off the counter in a move so swift that if he hadn't been watching, he might not have noticed.

He grinned. She was a sly one, his Sophia.

His eyes widened. Had he really just thought that?

She wasn't his.

He shouldn't be thinking that.

She made her way back to their corner and he didn't say anything about the way no one had said a word to her in all of that. All around them were voices, gossiping about their day, barking orders, and exclaiming about how little time they had left. But not a soul was paying attention to Sophia.

Not a soul except him.

A few of them had noticed him, though. He raised an eyebrow at Cook as she frowned at him. Cook didn't like him loitering in the kitchen, but what could she do?

Sophia unwrapped the butter she'd just finished wrapping, slicing off a small bit of it and spreading it on the bread. "Here you go," she said, sliding it over to him with a smile and reaching for her own tea.

Her fingers brushed his as she took the mug from him, and the corner of his lips turned up in a hint of a smile. "I'm sure that will be enough to hold you over until lunch," she said.

"I'm sure it will," he said. "Thank you."

"Of course," Sophia said with a smile. "I live to serve."

"I am very appreciative," he said, taking a large bite of the bread. It was still warm, and the butter was melting through it. He groaned aloud at the taste, and Sophia bit back a laugh, though part of it escaped anyway.

He wanted to do it again, if only to see that look on her face once more.

Laughter looked good on her. It was the first time since he'd arrived in the kitchen that he'd seen her light up like that.

How could everyone else not notice Sophia? She exuded a warm glow and happiness as she bustled around, making sure that everything was just so. She'd even offered him tea and bread before he'd mentioned he was hungry.

She was perfect.

Maybe that's what he was meant to be good at—noticing Sophia.

He looked at the girl across from him as she drank her tea, her eyes sparkling at him over the rim of her mug, her long, dark hair tumbling around her shoulders. It was usually tied up, probably so the goats wouldn't eat it.

He liked it down.

Of course, he thought it was pretty no matter how it was arranged. It was beautiful. She was beautiful.

And he was staring for far too long.

He took a sip of the tea and was surprised to find that it wasn't as bad as he thought it would be. It was actually rather good.

"Thank you for the tea and the food," he said. "I appreciate it very much."

"You're very welcome. I'll see you at lunch." She stood and took her mug with her. "I'm just going to go check on the goats."

He didn't know how to tell her that he wouldn't be at lunch with the rest of the servants and guards today, so he just nodded, though it was the coward's way out.

Caspian watched her leave, a sinking feeling in his chest growing as she walked away. He was starting to have feelings for her, and he was no closer to figuring out his plans for his future. He was going to hurt her, hurt himself, and he needed to stop.

He went to clean up before lunch with his family, and when he walked through the door of the dining room, his little sister launched herself at him with a squeal. "You came to lunch," she said, dragging him to the chair next to her. "Come sit with me."

There was a lump in his throat as he pushed Liliana's chair in for her before taking his own seat. He'd made Liliana happy, but Sophia would be looking for him, and he wouldn't be there.

He was stuck between two worlds, and he couldn't be in either one.

He needed to make a decision, and soon.

CHAPTER NINE
SOPHIA

SOPHIA'S STOMACH SANK AS she stared at Ivy. The grumpy, ornery goat was staring back, obviously plotting some sort of mischief.

"We have to get to the woods by the north pasture," Sophia said sternly. "You have to behave, or I'm going to leave you behind."

This wasn't going to end well.

The problem was, if she left Ivy, Tack, and Ned behind, they wouldn't stop hollering for her the entire time she was gone with the others.

She'd been asked to bring them to browse at the edge of the woods, and taking all seven of them was asking for trouble, but she didn't want to subject the rest of the manor to Ivy's frustration if she was left behind.

But really, she shouldn't be taking them to the woods by herself. It wouldn't do if she lost one of them because they got away from her.

Maybe Caspian was around. He and Liliana had joined her more than once in the past couple of weeks, and he was always willing to help. Her cheeks heated at the thought. It was flattering that he spent so much time with her...though she was still getting used to the idea of someone wanting to spend time with her.

It didn't seem real, and yet, somehow, it was. He was genuinely interested in spending time with her and had continued to seek her out since he'd arrived a few weeks ago.

The question was, how long would it last?

She narrowed her eyes at Ivy, hoping her stern demeanor would impart the seriousness of today's outing, before making her way outside the barn to look for Caspian.

If she didn't have help, she'd just have to leave some of the goats. She couldn't take all of them that far by herself, especially since there was no pen. They would be far too excited about getting to browse in the woods for her to manage all of them.

As Sophia scanned the courtyard, she found Caspian in the training yard, dueling with another guard. Her breath caught in her throat as he guarded himself against an attack, before moving to counterattack.

She'd never spent much time watching the guards dueling and training, but maybe she should have.

She walked closer, not wanting to startle him by calling his name, the details becoming clearer. Sweat beaded on his brow, his chest muscles straining against the confines of his sleeveless shirt, his biceps flexing with every move he made.

Sophia's mouth was dry, and she swallowed as the two men nodded at each other and lowered their swords. They broke into grins and clasped arms, pulling each other into a partial embrace as they congratulated each other on a fight well fought.

"Caspian," she called, and he immediately turned and smiled when he saw her.

Butterflies filled her stomach at his reaction.

"Would you be willing to help me with something?" she asked as the other guard turned to her also.

Caspian sheathed his sword and walked over to her. "That depends on what you need help with," he said, the corner of his mouth turning up.

The closer he got to her, the more she had a hard time breathing.

"I could help, miss," the other guard said, following behind Caspian.

"I think I've got it, Hopkins," Caspian said without turning around.

"Are you sure?"

"I've got it," Caspian said, taking a step closer to her.

"He's only trying to be helpful," Sophia said to Caspian, who was now so close she had to look up at him.

He took a deep breath, staring down at her with his dark brown eyes. "Thank you, Hopkins. I can help Miss Sophia. Thank you for the duel."

Sophia peeked around Caspian's frame and smiled at Hopkins. "Thank you, sir."

"Any time, miss," he said, nodding his head to her.

As he turned and walked away, Sophia frowned up at Caspian. "You didn't need to be rude to him," she pointed out.

Caspian shrugged. "That's how I am with him."

Sophia shook her head. "I hope he doesn't think he shouldn't talk to me now."

He reached out and brushed his hand down her arm. "If it would make you feel better, I'll let him know you appreciated his offer."

"Would you?" Sophia asked, allowing a smile to return to her face. "Thank you."

"Of course," Caspian said. "I'm sorry if I seemed rude. What can I help you with?"

In such close quarters, Sophia could smell the leather of his practice armor and a scent that was uniquely him. She'd been close to sweaty men before and had never found it to be a pleasant experience, but she had the urge to step even closer and sniff Caspian.

She took a step back to avoid such an embarrassing situation. "I was asked to bring the goats to clean up the woods to the north, but I can't bring all seven by myself. Would you like to go with me? We can pack lunch."

The mention of food was purely strategic, and she didn't miss the way his eyes lit up.

"Absolutely. Let me get cleaned up."

"I'll get the goats," she began.

"And I'll grab some food and meet you in the courtyard in twenty minutes," he said. "Does that sound like a plan?"

"Anything to avoid touching the goats," she teased. He rolled his eyes, but he smiled. "You know I'm right," she added when he didn't say anything. "Yes, that sounds like a good plan. Twenty minutes."

Sophia hurried into the barn to find the pack that she'd made for Ivy and put it on the doe, who twitched her ears in annoyance but held still long enough for her to fasten it. While Ivy seemed the most unlikely candidate for being their pack goat, she was the largest, and Sophia had discovered early on when trying to train them that she was least likely to try to get rid of it.

She added two flasks of water to the pack and put leads on all three of the does. Valley and Meadow probably didn't need them, but she couldn't wait to see Caspian's face when she handed him one of them.

The babies followed eagerly as she opened the gate and let all of them into the aisle. She held tight to Ivy's lead as they hurried toward the open door, and they burst into the courtyard with excitement.

They had only been there for a moment when Caspian came out of the kitchen with a bundle of food and a blanket tucked under one elbow. "I think this will be enough," he said, showing her the large bundle in his hand.

"I think that's enough food for an army," Sophia said.

"Having been part of the Royal Guard for two years, I can tell you it is not."

Sophia laughed as they put the food in Ivy's pack. "Yes, I suppose you would know better than I would. Here you go." She handed Ivy's lead to him, and he grimaced but took it. Though she noticed the way he carefully avoided brushing up against any of the goats.

It made her giggle to think about how he could be a guard for two years and presumably get fairly dirty during his training, but even touching a goat's lead rope made him grimace.

They began to walk north and soon they made it to the edge of the woods, where the stable master had asked her to let the goats browse. She could see why. It was overgrown with all sorts of brush that the goats would absolutely love.

Seeing it, too, the goats began pulling at their leads, eager to enjoy their favorite food.

"Let me get the pack off," Sophia said, letting go of Valley and Meadow and grabbing Ivy so she could take the pack from her. After a moment of wrestling with the clasp, she had it off, and she let go of the goat.

"You can let her go now," Sophia told Caspian, who dropped the lead rope as quickly as if it was on fire. Sensing her freedom, Ivy raced forward to join the other goats in the brush. "Couldn't wait to let go, hm?" she asked with a grin.

"Well, she seems perfectly well behaved this time, I didn't see a reason to keep holding once you told me I could let go," Caspian said as he spread out the blanket in the shade.

Eyeing the blanket, Sophia felt a surge of guilt for not asking Liliana if she wanted to come with them...but it was nice to spend time with Caspian without them having to watch her the whole time.

"She's only well behaved because you're here," Sophia said with a grin. "She likes you."

"Oh, joy," Caspian said, his nose wrinkling as he glanced over at Ivy.

Sophia laughed as she sat down on the blanket, leaving the pack off to the side so Caspian wouldn't have to worry about touching something that had touched the goats. She tucked her skirts in around her ankles to avoid an indecent situation and reached over to open the pack. "They won't go too far until they run out of food."

She pulled out two apples from the bundle that Caspian had brought and tossed one to him. "I love apples," she said happily as she took a bite of hers. The crisp, fall flavor burst on her tongue and she sighed in happiness. "They're one of my favorite fruits. Thank you for grabbing these."

"Do you like red or green apples better?" he asked before taking a bite of his own apple.

"Oh, red, definitely. I'm not a fan of green apples. They're a little too tart for me."

"Of course you like red apples—they're sweet, like you. I prefer the green apples," he said with a wink. "Fortunately for you, the kitchen had red apples in easy reach today."

"Did you eat green apples growing up?" she asked.

Caspian nodded as he finished the bite in his mouth. "Yes, growing up there was this tree that produced green apples, and it had low branches that my brothers and I used to climb. We would climb that tree for hours, and in the fall, we would gorge ourselves on apples. Mother always got mad because we would come back from playing outside and say we were too full to eat our dinner. She said she hated it, but I think she secretly loved it because we were having fun together. Even if it meant we didn't eat any of the food on our plate at dinner."

Sophia smiled. "That sounds like a lovely way to grow up. I wish I had siblings."

"Do you not have any?" he asked.

Sophia shook her head. "No. There were two maids that were my same age in the household where I worked, but they didn't want to talk to me much, because Lady Manning didn't like me. I had Rosaleen, the cook, who was almost like a mother to me, but I was alone as far as I know."

"You didn't know your parents," he said.

Sophia looked away. She didn't want to see the sympathy on his face.

"No," Sophia said softly. "I don't know anything about my family. All I remember is the way she seemed to hate me."

"Is that why you had to leave?" he asked quietly.

Sophia sighed and picked a blade of grass to fidget with. "Yes. She never liked me, but as I got older, it changed for the worse. Rosaleen grew worried that it wouldn't take much for her to snap and hurt me—or worse. She wanted me to leave, to be safe."

She looked up, but Caspian wouldn't make eye contact with her.

This was why she didn't tell anyone about her past.

"I'm sorry. I shouldn't have brought it up," she began, but he reached over and took her hand in his.

"That sounds terrible," he said. "I'm so sorry that was your life until now. I hope you've found things to be better here."

Sophia stared down at their joined hands, a warm glow spreading through her. "I have all my friends at the café, and everyone at the manor is perfectly nice to me. They don't talk to me much, but I'd rather be quiet in the corner than dead."

Caspian let out a snort. "I suppose that's the better option. I do wish you had friends here at the manor, though."

"I have you," she said softly, looking up at him.

When did he get so close?

His arm wrapped around her waist, and she leaned in closer, melting into his embrace.

This was the most wonderful feeling she had ever felt in her entire life.

Caspian's dark eyes met hers as he leaned in closer. Was he going to kiss her? What did you do when someone was going to kiss you? She'd never been kissed before, never been this close to a man before, never even touched a man like this before.

She closed her eyes as he closed the distance between them, and his free hand slid up her other arm, and then something landed in her lap and knocked her off-balance.

She opened her eyes as she landed flat on her back with baby Mollie on top of her, head-butting her in the face. "What just happened?" she asked, giggling as Caspian collapsed next to her shaking with laughter.

"The baby goat happened," Caspian said, still laughing.

"I've never had that happen before," she said.

"You've never had a baby goat stop someone from kissing you before?" he asked, rolling onto his side to look at her.

She stared up at the sky, avoiding his gaze. "This is the first time anyone's ever tried to kiss me."

Caspian let out a disbelieving noise. She turned onto her side to look at him, knocking Mollie off. He reached over and tucked a strand of hair behind her ear, smoothing it out of her face. "I would like to kiss you someday."

Sophia's cheeks burned, but she felt the same way. "I would like to kiss you someday, too," she said, almost in a whisper.

She'd never really considered kissing anyone before, but suddenly she was overwhelmed with the urge to kiss Caspian.

His eyes held hers captive. "Do you think next time, we could avoid bringing the baby goats along?"

Sophia giggled. "I think that could probably be arranged."

"Hey now," Caspian said loudly, rolling onto his back and sitting up abruptly. "What do you think you're doing?"

Sophia looked over to see Mollie letting go of his sleeve, which showed clear signs of being nibbled by the baby goat. She grinned as she realized they'd been distracted enough for Mollie to get close enough to try to eat him. "Having a problem?" she asked, trying to contain her laughter and failing.

"She's trying to eat me," Caspian said, glaring down at the baby goat.

"She only has bottom teeth, she can't eat you," Sophia explained, the words coming out between chuckles. "I promise, you and your shirt will both survive this experience."

He turned to her with a pained look. "It's wet."

"Yes, that's what happens when fabric enters something's mouth."

"It's goat slobber. On my sleeve."

Sophia shook her head. "I should have known this would be difficult for you."

He narrowed his eyes at her, his lips turning up into a smirk. "And you think it's funny."

"I'm sorry," she said, fighting to hide her smile.

"Do you want to go for a walk tonight?" he asked. "Without any interrupting trouble-makers straggling along?"

"I think that sounds like a great plan," Sophia said as butterflies filled her stomach.

Did that mean he was going to kiss her tonight?

"I agree," he said softly.

And then there was a splash of water on her nose.

And another. And one bouncing off his forehead.

Sophia looked up and the skies above the trees were dark. "I didn't think it was going to rain," she said. She jumped to her feet. "The goats hate rain. We need to grab them."

They hurried to put the lead ropes back on the goats and they trudged home through the rain, the goats setting a faster pace than usual. Sophia wasn't sure who hated the rain and mud more, Caspian or the goats. Not that she was a fan of it, either.

"I suppose this means no walk tonight," Sophia said as they entered the courtyard and the goats immediately tried to run for their barn.

"No walk tonight," Caspian agreed as they entered the barn. His gaze dropped to her lips, and even though Sophia had never been so cold and wet in her entire life, she suddenly felt like she was on fire. "But soon. I promise."

Chapter Ten
Caspian

Caspian whistled a merry tune as he sauntered into the dining room for breakfast and found his usual seat, watching as his father pulled out his mother's chair for her.

His mother smiled up at Lord Rendon with a "thank you, my love," and Caspian shook his head at their sappy display. Their love was still apparent, even after nearly thirty years.

He wanted that. And he was pretty sure he wanted it with Sophia.

Liliana leaned over and tugged on his shirt. "Caspian, will you come play with me today?" she asked. "I'm having a tea party."

He looked down at his little sister with a smile. "I suppose I could do that. I do have to go into town for more festival work today, but maybe before or after that, we could have a tea party."

His mother smiled approvingly from her end of the table. His brothers snickered across from him, but he didn't care. Kellan and Gideon could tease him all they wanted. It turned out, tea wasn't actually that bad, and spending time with his sister would make his mother happy. So having a tea party, while it might not have been at the top of his list, suddenly seemed like a not so terrible thing.

Maybe he could even convince Liliana to make it a tea party with the goats and get Sophia involved. The thought of Ivy presiding over a tea party made him grin, as did the thought of enjoying the afternoon with Sophia.

Yes, a tea party seemed like a splendid idea.

"What are you working on for the festival today?" Lady Rendon asked, turning to him. "You don't have much time left."

No, he didn't, given that the festival was the following day.

"Final attempts to coordinate music and the bonfire," he said. "I got the vendors sorted out over the past week, but I'm still trying to figure out who plays what instruments, and if I can get enough of them to have dancing."

"I love dancing," his mother exclaimed, looking over at Lord Rendon with a big smile.

"Promise you'll save a dance for me?" Lord Rendon asked.

"I'll save you as many as you want."

"You might regret that." Lord Rendon winked at his wife, and Caspian's brothers made pretend gagging noises.

It may have been a little over the top, but Caspian thought it was wonderful having parents who still loved each other so much.

"I think dancing is a great idea," his mother said, turning back to him. "Perhaps all of you will find someone to dance with at the festival." She eyed all three of her sons, and Caspian grinned as his brothers turned pale.

"Maybe," Caspian said. Could his mother tell that he had someone in mind?

Clearly, his brothers didn't.

"Please let me know if you need any help with anything," Lady Rendon said.

Caspian shook his head. "No, thank you. I don't want you to worry about it on the last day. Maybe you should join us for the tea party instead."

Kellan snickered across the table.

"Would you like to join us, too?" Caspian asked, turning to him.

His brother shook his head. "No thanks. I'm busy today."

"Me, too," Gideon piped up.

"Are you sure?" Liliana asked, her face pleading as she looked at her older brothers.

Kellan's face softened as he looked at his sister. "I can't today, Little Bit, but maybe after Caspian goes back to Riyel I'll have a tea party with you."

His sister's face grew somber. "I don't want Caspian to go back to Riyel."

"I know," Caspian said, reaching over and pulling her into a hug. "I don't want to go back, either."

"You should stay," she said, looking up at him with a big grin.

"We'll see, Little Bit," Caspian said. "I'm going to go to town and see about my tasks, and when I get back, I'll have a tea party with you."

"Yes, please," Liliana said, bouncing up and down in her chair.

"Finish your oatmeal," he said, pointing to the offending dish.

"If I must," Liliana said, turning back to her mostly full bowl and tucking into it.

Caspian wiped his face with his napkin and stood, nodding to his mother and father before taking his leave. Maybe he could see if Sophia wanted to go to town with him and ask her opinion on having a tea party with the goats.

He pounded his way down the stairs to the kitchen, hoping to find Sophia, but she wasn't there. He didn't want to ask for her and draw attention to the fact that he was looking for her, so he poked his head into the storage room in case she was in there.

He didn't see her at first glance, but there was a stack of apple crates, and he could see movement behind them. He made his way around them, and there she was.

"Sophia," he said quietly, hoping she wouldn't be scared by an unexpected person appearing. When she turned to see him, her eyes lit up, and joy rushed through him.

She was happy to see him, just as he was happy to see her.

"Good morning," she said, standing from the overturned crate she was sitting on. "What are you doing here?"

"I have to go to town," he said. "Will you walk with me?"

Sophia glanced down at the open crate on the floor. "I'm supposed to sort the apples," she said. "I don't want to get in trouble."

"I won't let you get in trouble."

"I don't know," she said, concern filling her eyes.

"I promise," he said. He reached out and took her hand, pulling her out of the storage room. He wove his way through the chaos to tap Cook on the shoulder. "I need Sophia to come to town with me," he announced. "Oh, and Liliana wants a tea party this afternoon. I said I'd let you know."

He towed her out of the kitchen before Cook could respond, but she wouldn't say no.

She couldn't.

"You just told her what you were doing," Sophia said in wonder, as they began to walk down to the front gate.

Apparently Sophia hadn't spent much time with nobility.

Leaves fluttered to the ground as they walked through the trees near the gate and began the walk to town. The sun was shining, and he held her hand the whole time. He couldn't stop smiling.

It felt so right.

He didn't know why it felt so right, but he didn't want to let it go. He wanted to do more than hold her hand—he wanted to kiss her. But the moment didn't feel right, and he wasn't going to do it until the moment felt right.

Sophia's first kiss needed to be perfect.

He had a plan, though. The Fall Festival seemed like a pretty perfect moment to him, especially if they managed to pull it off together. So as much as he wanted to kiss her now, he was going to wait, and it was going to be even better for waiting.

Even if the waiting might kill him.

Every day he spent with Sophia only strengthened his resolve that she was the one for him. He couldn't imagine leaving her to go find some wealthy lady to marry. The very idea of it sickened him, and that feeling was only growing stronger the more time he spent with her.

He needed to talk to his parents.

They arrived at the library, and he discussed the Fall Festival with Beatrice at the front desk while Sophia perused the books on the shelves.

"If there's one you want to take home, Sophia," Beatrice called out to her, "feel free to do so. I'll put it on your account."

"I don't have an account," Sophia said, "and I have no way of putting up any money for the books."

Beatrice shook her head. "That's not necessary. All you have to do is promise to bring it back. And if something happens to it, just let me know and we'll figure it out together."

Sophia smiled and turned back to the shelves, and Caspian took a moment to watch her look at all the books. She looked so peaceful browsing through the shelves in her dress and apron, which he hadn't given her time to take off before pulling her away from her work.

Oh, well. It looked good on her.

The library door opened and the two old ladies from before entered. They probably haunted the library just to see him.

"How are you today, ladies?" he asked, hoping to head them off before they got too vocal about how much they liked him and how much they wanted him to save a dance for them at the Fall Festival.

"Oh, it's the lovely Caspian," one of them said, clapping in delight.

Which lady it was, he wasn't sure. But he was sure they'd tell him.

"It's a pleasure to see you both." He bowed in respect.

"So charming," the other one said as they giggled to each other.

"Can I help you find any books?" Beatrice asked pointedly.

"Oh, no, darling, we were just coming in to see if, well, to see if—" She faltered, and her companion stepped up helpfully.

"We just wanted to come say hello to you, that's all," she said.

"Well, hello, Eugenia," Beatrice said patiently. "I hope you're having a great day."

Caspian's gaze slid to Sophia, who looked thoroughly amused by the situation, and back to the old ladies. But they'd noticed he was distracted, and they winked at him in unison, which was odd.

"I see there's someone who's caught your eye," Eugenia said in a knowing voice.

Caspian refused to look at Sophia. He didn't want to see the look on her face.

"You ladies have a wonderful day," he said, doing his best to dismiss them before they could say anything else.

"Oh, you, too," they said, smirking at him as they turned and left.

"Those two are something else," Beatrice said with a laugh.

Caspian smiled and shook his head. "I'm glad I can amuse."

"I think they just appreciate having a handsome young man to tease," Beatrice said.

Caspian quirked an eyebrow. "They said I'm handsome?"

Beatrice chuckled. "Of course Eugenia said you're attractive. But lest you think you're special, they say that about every man in the town under the age of sixty—and most of the ones older than that."

Caspian laughed at the thought of the ladies chasing after some of the older men in the village. "They certainly make life more interesting. Now, enough about that—back to the plans. I was hoping to ask every family who came to bring a log of wood for the bonfire. What do you think of that?"

Beatrice shook her head. "No, I wouldn't do that. I think we should ask if any of the nobility would like to donate wood for the bonfire. I can send a message if you'd like. The townspeople will pay for their own food and drink, but I try not to burden them with any of the expenses for the festival, so they can just enjoy the evening. The nobility are happy to help most of the time."

She seemed to realize who she was talking to then and looked up at him sheepishly. "Sorry for being so blunt."

He shook his head. "I appreciate the honesty. I can't learn what I don't know if nobody tells me."

"That is true," Beatrice said.

The library door opened, and they turned to see Dietrich come in. Caspian fought the urge to groan. Of course it was the one man in town who disliked him the most.

"Sophia," Dietrich called. "Thea wants to see you."

Sophia looked over at Caspian. "I'll be at the café," she told him, already hurrying to the door.

Dietrich held it open for her and gave Caspian a look that he couldn't quite decipher as the door shut behind them.

"I take it Dietrich is not a fan of you courting Sophia," Beatrice said with a grin.

"Apparently not," Caspian said with a sigh. "I don't know what I did, but he seems determined not to like me."

"Dietrich is very protective of Sophia. You'll win him over."

Caspian frowned at the stack of bookmarks on the desk. "I know, because Sophia cares about Dietrich's opinion. I'll have to change his mind somehow."

Like that wasn't a tall order.

But like it or not, Sophia looked up to the man, and he needed to be on good terms with him if he wanted to win over Sophia.

And he definitely wanted to win over Sophia.

So he was going to have to win over Dietrich.

Chapter Eleven

Sophia

Sophia followed Dietrich out of the library, glancing over her shoulder before she left.

Caspian was watching her leave.

She grinned at the thought as they started across the village square. Dietrich's legs were shorter than Caspian's, so walking with him was easier, but somehow it wasn't as enjoyable.

She was looking forward to returning home with Caspian.

Dietrich looked over at her. "I don't know how much you know about Caspian," he said shortly. "But I want you to make sure that you're being careful."

So Dietrich had finally decided to address the situation instead of just glaring at Caspian.

It would be good to clear the air.

"Why do you think I need to be careful?" she asked. "I haven't seen anything thus far that would lead me to believe there could be a problem with Caspian."

Dietrich tilted his head. "I don't know why, but I don't like him."

Dietrich was a lot of things, but he wasn't a trusting man.

"You don't like anybody," Sophia teased. "Why would you like him?"

He gave a rueful chuckle. "I suppose you're right, I don't like anybody, but still."

Sophia smiled softly. "I'm sorry that you don't like him," she said. "But I think he deserves a fair chance. And I don't want to discount him entirely because you don't like him."

Dietrich grinned. "That's fair. I just don't want to see you hurt." He slung an arm around her shoulders as they approached the front door of the café. "You know that, right?"

He was the older brother she'd never had. The way he acted with her...it felt the way she'd always imagined a sibling relationship would be.

Sophia elbowed him in the ribs. "Yes, I do. Thank you for being like a brother to me and always looking out for me. Just...look out for me with a little less glaring, please?"

Dietrich laughed. "If you say so, little sister. I'll do my best."

As they stepped up to the front door, Dietrich let go of her shoulders and opened the door for her. The bell jingled as Sophia's senses were assailed with the smell of warm spices and the sounds of cheerful people.

The café had a few people scattered around enjoying a meal, and Sophia smiled at Thea, who was bustling around behind the counter.

"You sit," Dietrich told her, gesturing toward a seat near the fireplace. "I'll grab our drinks and Thea."

"I can get my drink," she protested, reaching into her apron pocket, her hand coming out empty.

Dietrich smirked. "Sure you can."

Sophia sighed and made her way to her usual seat. Sensing her arrival, Ginger promptly appeared, and Sophia scooped her up. The pretty orange kitty snuggled into her lap and fell asleep after only a moment of purring.

Satisfaction filled her bones as the warm weight of the sleeping cat lulled her.

She hadn't slept well the night before, tossing and turning with a sense of dread.

It didn't make sense. Everything was going well, and yet, she was more uneasy than she had been in months.

Sitting here with Ginger always made her feel better.

Dietrich arrived with two drinks and handed one of them to Sophia.

"You didn't need to do that," she said halfheartedly. "I would have been fine."

"We're supporting Thea," Dietrich said, sitting down next to her and leaning back in his seat.

"Is supporting Thea the only thing you do?" she teased.

"No, it's not," he said pointedly. "You know I work for Duke Vaught."

"And yet it seems like you're always in town."

He shook his head. "The Duke is still in Riyel with his new family. There are only a few of us on the estate, and there's not much to do without the family in residence. Besides, they ran things fine before the Duke sent me here. They don't need me for much."

"And it's more fun to be in town than on the estate?" Sophia asked.

"Especially when you're here to tease," Dietrich said.

Sophia took a sip of her cinnamon honey coffee and relaxed further into her seat. "If you must," she said, "I'll allow it."

"I would hope so, given that I did save your life," he pointed out.

"Are you going to hold that over my head for the rest of my life?"

"The life that you're able to live because I saved you? Yes. Yes, I am."

Sophia grinned as he leaned over and shoved her shoulder with his. "I suppose that's fair."

There was a clatter as something fell to the floor and Sophia and Dietrich turned to glance at Thea.

"Here, let me help," a man said, hurrying around the counter.

"Thank you, Nathaniel, but I can handle it," Thea said stiffly.

Sophia raised an eyebrow at the tension in Thea's voice. It was unlike her.

"You don't have to do it all alone," Nathaniel said, his voice so quiet she could barely hear him.

"I am quite capable of handling it," Thea said. "Thank you though." The man left the kitchen and Sophia looked at Dietrich, who shrugged and shook his head.

He didn't know what was going on, either.

"Can I do anything for you?" Nathaniel asked in a normal voice as he paid for his drink.

"No, thank you, everything in the building is perfect," Thea said, her voice returned to her normal tone. "Now if you'll excuse me, I need to speak to Dietrich and Sophia."

"Anything for you," he said.

Before Sophia could say anything to Dietrich about the confusing conversation they'd just overheard, Thea joined them, sitting down with a sigh. "Busy morning," she said.

"I could have helped," Dietrich said.

"I was fine," Thea said, waving a hand dismissively. "I wanted to see Sophia for myself, and you fetched her."

"What's wrong?" Sophia asked, taking in the worry lines etched on Thea's rich brown features. Her black, curly hair, usually tied back in a neat style, blew freely around her face, and Thea reached up to brush back an errant curl.

"I haven't slept well the past couple of nights worrying about you," Thea admitted. "I wanted to see if you were well."

Sophia shrugged. "I haven't slept well, either, but all is well."

Thea nodded, the worry lines easing slightly. "I had hoped to hear that. Maybe I'll sleep better tonight."

"Please don't lose sleep on my account," Sophia said, setting her drink down on the low table in front of her and leaning forward to look at Thea directly, as much as she could with the warm lump of a cat occupying her lap. "You've done so much for me, and I could never repay you. Either of you." She glanced at Dietrich.

"We would do it all over again," he said lazily.

Dietrich reminded her of a cat himself, the way he liked to sit in the sunshine, sprawl back, and do nothing. Though he'd be a light tan tabby cat, short-haired and scrappy, rather than the spoiled, long-haired orange feline currently warming Sophia's legs.

"Yes, we would," Thea said. "I am so glad to see you've settled into Lord Rendon's estate so nicely. I thought you would forever be nervous as a rabbit, but you seem to have found your place there and it makes me happy."

Dietrich chuckled. "Sophia is a rabbit. Yes, that makes sense."

"You're a cat," Sophia said, shrugging one shoulder.

"A what?" he asked, raising one eyebrow at her.

"You can't even be bothered to sit up," Sophia pointed out, looking between him and Ginger. "Yes, you're a cat."

"What does that make Thea?" Dietrich asked.

"A honeybee," Sophia said promptly. The answer appeared in her head without any hesitation.

"I could see it," Dietrich mused, rubbing his hand over his chin as he stared at Thea. "Though she looks more like a bumblebee."

"Enough animals," Thea said in exasperation, flapping her hands at him. "I was trying to lead Sophia to tell us more about her past and you're rambling on about me being a bumblebee."

Sophia glanced at Thea, instinctively reaching for her mug again to have something to hold onto. "What do you want to know?" she asked warily.

Thea stared steadily at her. "Anything you want to tell us," she said softly. "I don't want you to keep holding it in. I know the danger of holding everything in."

Dietrich raised his eyebrow again. "Are you suggesting you have your own dark, mysterious past, Thea?"

Sophia thought of the conversation a few moments ago that felt like there were hidden layers. Did her past involve Nathaniel?

The older woman shifted her attention to him. "And what of it, Dietrich? Would you like me to pry into your history?"

Muttering something under his breath, Dietrich shook his head, gesturing back to Sophia.

Sophia considered what she might tell them. They'd surely proved worthy of her trust…so why did she find it so hard to tell them what her life had been like before she'd arrived in the Northlands, nearly frozen to death?

"I was mistreated at my former home," she said simply. "The cook, who was like a mother to me, grew worried that the lady of the home was becoming a danger to my safety, so she urged me to leave and find somewhere new. I was ill prepared for the journey, and, well, you know the rest."

They knew how Dietrich had found her, nearly frozen to death in the snow, and had brought her to Thea. They'd been the ones to find her a home with Lord Rendon, and she owed everything to them.

Thea gave her a soft smile. "Thank you for trusting us with your past. I know how hard that can be."

"We're always here if you wish to share your own," Sophia said quietly.

The bell over the door jingled and Caspian and Beatrice walked in. Thea sprang to her feet and hurried behind the counter, the conversation effectively over.

"I know curiosity killed the cat, and yet, I find myself very curious," Dietrich said quietly.

"I agree," Sophia said, her gaze following Thea as she greeted Beatrice at the counter.

But there wasn't time to pry into Thea's past, because Caspian was standing in front of her. Her heart skipped a beat when he smiled.

Dietrich was wary about him, but Dietrich didn't like anyone.

He made her happy, and he made her feel safe—how could this be wrong?

"Are you ready to go?" he asked, offering a hand.

"I'll have to move the cat," Sophia said, regret lacing her words. "Sorry, Ging." She leaned over and kissed the top of the cat's head before picking her up and moving her to Dietrich's lap.

"I don't want her," Dietrich protested.

"You're stuck," Sophia said with a grin as she accepted Caspian's hand and let him help her to her feet. "Thanks for the drink."

"You owe me one," he responded.

"Of course," Sophia said. "Next time I actually plan to come to town and remember my purse, I'll be sure to get you one."

"I'm sure you'll continue to conveniently forget your money," Dietrich teased as she followed Caspian out the door, though not before turning and sticking her tongue out at Dietrich.

The walk through town was quiet, and Caspian was back to walking at a faster pace, but she didn't mind.

Thea's concern for her was touching, but she had to admit, she was just as curious as Dietrich about Thea's past now.

She hadn't spent much time considering it before. Surely Thea and the Cozy Cat Café had always been a staple in town. But maybe they hadn't been.

She'd always known that Dietrich preferred to pretend the past didn't exist...but Thea?

At least Dietrich had finally addressed the fact that he didn't trust Caspian. His concern was touching, but she couldn't help that she was falling for Caspian, and he had given her no reasons not to trust him.

Had she just thought that she was falling for him?

The thought made her heart race even more than the fast pace did.

Was she really?

She couldn't possibly be falling for him already.

She was being silly.

Trusting him was one thing. Falling for him was another entirely.

It was time to learn how to trust again. Thea and Dietrich had been good practice. Now she could start opening up to people at the manor.

If Caspian was first on the list, well, that was just how it was.

"I don't suppose you like persimmons," Caspian said out of the blue.

"Persimmons?" she asked, her nose wrinkling.

"You've never had a persimmon?" he asked.

She shook her head. "I don't know what that is."

He gasped. "You don't have those in the city?"

"I'm afraid not," she said with a wry grin. "I still don't know what it is."

Caspian sighed. "This is a tragedy. We must rectify this wrong."

Sophia laughed as he took her hand and pulled her off the path toward a straggly tree a few yards away. Once they reached the tree, he squatted, searching the ground for something.

The ground was littered with squashed orange fruit, speckled with browns and blacks.

They looked disgusting.

"Here you go," Caspian said, offering her the nastiest one she'd seen yet.

Sophia frowned. "You want me to eat that?"

He nodded his head with a grin. "I know it seems strange, but trust me, the ugliest looking persimmons are always the most delicious ones. There are seeds in there, so make sure you don't eat them."

"You go first," she said, her nose wrinkling again. Would it really be tragic if she never ate one of these persimmon things?

Caspian plopped the fruit in his mouth and moaned in appreciation. "It's so good," he said after spitting out the seeds. "Can I get you one, please?"

She narrowed her eyes at him, but didn't say anything, and he knelt down and found a few more of the fruit.

She did not want to try it.

He offered them to her, and she picked one up, staring at it suspiciously before the tip of her tongue poked out and touched an exposed portion of the fruit where the skin was broken.

It wasn't instantly terrible.

She waited a moment, letting the taste sit on her tongue, before deciding she could attempt a small bite.

"I don't suppose you've ever had anything like it before," he said. "What do you think?"

"It tastes a little like...pumpkin?" she asked. "It's not as good. But it's not bad."

"Persimmon is one of my favorite fall flavors," he said.

"It's good, I think," she said, taking another small nibble of the fruit.

"Just pop the whole thing in your mouth, seeds and all, and then you spit them out and it grows more trees." He demonstrated, popping a whole persimmon in his mouth.

"Is your goal to have an entire persimmon forest one day?" she teased before popping a whole fruit in her mouth.

"You bet." He watched as she worked the fruit with her tongue, separating the seeds from the flesh before spitting the seeds out.

"That's not too bad." She took another one from his hand.

"I told you," he said with a grin. "Now, if you get a perfect-looking one, don't eat it. They're terribly astringent and will make your entire mouth pucker."

"Really?" she asked, frowning at him. That seemed far-fetched.

"Absolutely," he said. "If you don't trust me, you could try one."

She laughed and shook her head. "No, thank you. I trust you."

The words spilled out and her breath caught in her throat at how easy it was.

He offered his arm, and she took it as they continued walking toward the manor. The touch and closeness made her warm all over, and it didn't hurt that holding his arm offered a reminder to slow down with his long legs.

"Can I ask you a favor?" he asked.

She looked up at him and raised her eyebrows.

"Can we have a tea party with Mollie?" he asked.

Sophia laughed. "I was not expecting that."

Caspian grinned. "Liliana is having a tea party this afternoon," he explained, "and I thought it would be fun to surprise her with a baby goat."

"You've spent time with the goats before, right?" Sophia asked. "You remember how certain baby goats feel about people sitting on the ground together?"

His dark eyes burned into hers at the reminder of their almost kiss and he stopped walking. "I do," he said, his voice suddenly husky. But then he glanced ahead of them, where the walls of the manor were in sight, and he straightened. "I remember," he added. "But it would make Liliana happy."

Sophia let out a chuckle. "Well, since keeping Liliana happy is a large part of my job description, how can I say no?"

"I was hoping you'd say that," he said, looking back down at her, the teasing light back in his eyes. "I'll talk to Cook."

"May I suggest mugs that won't break easily," Sophia said.

"I think that's probably a good idea," he said with a grin.

Sophia's heart kicked into overdrive as they finished their walk and he deposited her in front of the barn. He winked before turning away and Sophia took a deep breath.

She was falling, and she was falling hard.

As long as he was there to help break her fall...surely it couldn't be that bad.

Chapter Twelve
CASPIAN

CASPIAN MADE HIS WAY into the kitchen to speak to Cook about the tea party.

"Sophia has been pulled to help with Liliana's tea party," he informed her. "Will you have things prepared for that soon? I have to get a blanket for the courtyard."

"Why are you having tea in the courtyard?" Cook asked, frowning at him.

"Because we're having a baby goat join us," he said.

Her eyes widened. "A baby goat tea party? You're willingly eating with an animal?"

Yes, it was out of character for him, but she didn't have to act so surprised.

"For Liliana," he said.

And because it was an excuse for Sophia to join him.

Not at all because he wanted to have a tea party with a goat.

"Can you prepare enough for at least three of us, maybe more?" he asked.

Cook huffed, but she adored Liliana. She wouldn't say no.

"You're the best," he said, patting her on the shoulder as he hurried toward the door and made his way through the manor to the family's wing.

"Lil?" he called as he entered the schoolroom. "Are you in here?"

Liliana looked up from the book she was reading and squealed. "You came for me," she cried, dropping her book and running at him. "Please tell me we can have a tea party," she said. "I'm tired of reading this book."

Caspian grinned. "How about a tea party with a goat?" he asked.

Liliana's shriek of excitement was probably loud enough to be heard through the entire manor.

"You've got to get dressed," Caspian said, surveying the frilly dress she wore. "I know Mollie will decimate that dress in a matter of moments if she gets anywhere near it."

"What does decimate mean?" Liliana asked.

"Destroy."

Liliana nodded, running her fingers along the fine lace that edged her sleeves. "Yes, you're right, she would absolutely decimate this dress. Do you think my red dress is dressy enough for a tea party but not too dressy for Mollie?"

Caspian frowned. "I don't know," he said, not sure how to tell her that he had absolutely no idea what dress she was talking about.

"I'm gonna go look," she said, running out of the schoolroom, nearly colliding with Kellan on her way out the door.

"What's happening in here?"

Caspian grinned. "I told Little Bit it was time for our tea party. She's a little excited."

Kellan sighed. "I'm glad you're spending time with her. She misses you, you know."

"I know." Caspian shrugged, raising his hands. "But what can you do? I can't take back being in Riyel for the past two years. All I can do is try to make up for it now."

His brother shifted and crossed his arms across his chest. "Well, it's good that you're home now. We all missed you."

Caspian put his hand up to his ear. "I'm sorry, what was that?"

"I missed you, you idiot," his brother said, shaking his head. "You're such a pain."

"And yet, you missed me," Caspian said with a grin.

"Yeah, yeah, I already said it once, don't make me say it again."

"Say what again?" their other brother asked, appearing in the doorway.

"Kellan said he missed me," Caspian said.

"Wait, he admitted he has feelings?" Gideon said with a gasp. "I can't believe it."

"Oh, shut up," Kellan said, shoving Gideon.

"Such a touching moment," Caspian said with fake emotion in his voice, pressing his hand to his chest. "If only our mother had been here to see it."

"You tell her and I'll lop your head off," Kellan threatened. "I'm doing perfectly well convincing Mother that I'm not ready for a wife, even if I am past the ripe old age of twenty-five. She finds out I admitted to having feelings about my brother coming home and she'll start sending out the matchmakers."

"It must be so difficult being the heir," Gideon said mockingly. "All the glory and honor and the title."

"All the responsibility, hard work, and heartache," Kellan said seriously. "I envy you boys sometimes, you know?"

Gideon sobered up. "Yeah, I know. I don't take for granted the fact that I don't have that responsibility. Even if it seems like you have it easier than us sorry sods most of the time."

"Yeah, well, I'm the one trying to build up the estate enough to give you two any sort of land, so you should consider that next time you try to make fun of me."

Caspian stared at his brother. "You're trying to give us land?"

Kellan shrugged. "I don't feel right taking all of it. It depends on who you marry, obviously, but I'd like to be able to give you something if you need it. We'll see how long Father retains the title and how the next couple of years change the estate, but it's my goal."

"That's awfully nice of you," Gideon said, elbowing Kellan. "Thanks."

"Now if you'd just stop disappearing all the time," Kellan told Gideon pointedly.

"I have my reasons," Gideon said, meeting his brother's eyes steadily. "I've told you."

"And yet, we still don't know what they are," Kellan said.

"I don't enjoy keeping secrets," Gideon said quietly. "If I could tell you, I would."

"I know," Kellan said. His voice was heavy. "Which worries me."

Caspian barely heard any of their discussion, his mind caught up in the fact that Kellan was hoping to give his brothers land. If he got a piece of land, maybe he could marry Sophia and stay here.

It would make his mother happy, Sophia wouldn't have to go back to Riyel with its painful memories, and he would be with Sophia.

Everyone would be satisfied.

Footsteps hurried down the hall and Liliana ran back into the room in a red dress, her expression growing even happier as she took in the fact that all three of her brothers were standing in her schoolroom. "Are you all coming to my tea party?" she asked.

"Oh, no," Kellan said. "I just came to see how pretty you looked before you got to spend time with Caspian."

Smooth, Kellan. Nice job.

He winked at Caspian over Liliana's head as she gave him a hug.

"You look absolutely beautiful, Lil," Gideon said.

"I know," she said, pulling away from Kellan to twirl in a circle. "I thought this dress would be perfect."

It did look perfect, or at least as perfect as a dress could look when Mollie was involved.

"Are you ready?" Caspian asked, offering his arm to Liliana.

"Not yet," she said, taking his hand and tugging him toward his brothers. "Group hug first."

The three men grumbled as their baby sister pulled them all into a group hug, throwing her arms around Caspian and Kellan. But Caspian had to admit, as he put his arm around Gideon's shoulders and squished his little sister, this wasn't terrible.

As far as siblings went, he was pretty lucky.

"Now I'm ready," Liliana said, her face glowing as she took a step back and reached for Caspian's arm.

"Well, then, right this way, my lady," he said, offering his arm, having to bend over a bit for her to reach it.

Kellan and Gideon smirked at him as he hobbled away with Liliana and he made a rude gesture behind his back, which sent both of them into peals of laughter.

"I'm so excited for our tea party," Liliana said as they made their way to the kitchen. When they arrived, they were greeted with the welcome sight of a picnic basket, complete with a blanket on top of it.

"Thank you," Caspian called to Cook. He snagged the basket as Liliana towed him out of the kitchen at a breakneck pace. "Slow down, Little Bit. You're gonna wreck us."

Liliana must not have heard him, because as they stepped into the courtyard and she saw Mollie, she only moved faster.

Caspian smiled at the image of Sophia in the courtyard with Mollie, attempting to hold the baby goat, who only wanted to get down. When she heard Liliana coming, she let Mollie go with a sigh of relief, and the goat ran to Liliana.

"Hello," Caspian said to Sophia, as if he hadn't just seen her less than an hour ago.

"Hello," she replied, her cheeks turning a delicious shade of pink.

"We're going to have a tea party," Liliana told Sophia, bounding up to her and grabbing her arm. "Thank you so much for bringing Mollie."

"Of course," Sophia said, watching as Caspian spread the blanket on the grass in the courtyard. "I suppose we should help set out the party, shouldn't we?"

"Of course, that's my job as the hostess," Liliana said matter-of-factly, and Caspian and Sophia looked at each other with laughter in their eyes.

"Such a serious eight-year-old hostess," he said.

"I'm almost nine," she protested.

"Keep telling yourself that, Little Bit," he said, reaching over to rub her hair.

"Don't touch," she said, glaring at him.

"Sorry, I won't touch," he said, raising his hands in innocence as they sat down on the blanket. "Do you want to serve, or should we let Sophia be the hostess?"

"Sophia can do it," Liliana said begrudgingly, reaching over to pet Mollie.

Sophia reached into the basket, pulling out a flask of tea, three metal mugs, and a wrapped plate. When she unwrapped the plate, it revealed an arrangement of meat, cheese, bread, fruits, and vegetables. A delicious spread, all on one manageable plate.

"Cook outdid herself," Caspian said as Liliana immediately took a piece of cheese and bread.

Sophia poured the tea into each mug and when he took his from her, his fingers brushed against hers. She gave him a tiny smile, as if she was hoping Liliana wouldn't see it, and he wanted to do it again.

Alas, it wouldn't make sense to hand his mug back and take it again so he could brush his hand against hers...but he'd be lying if he said he wasn't considering it.

Sophia reached for a red apple slice, and he smiled as he took a green one, remembering their discussion on the best types of apples.

"What do you suppose we should talk about at a tea party with a goat?" Caspian asked, turning to his little sister.

"We could talk about how perfectly normal it is to eat food with a goat," Sophia teased with a mischievous glint in her eyes.

"Or we could discuss how said baby goat completely wandered away from us?" he told her, tilting his head.

Sophia's eyes widened and she turned to see Hopkins approaching with Mollie under one arm. "Oh, thank you for getting her," she said. "I got distracted pouring the tea."

Caspian smirked.

"Of course, miss," Hopkins said.

"Are you hungry, Hopkins?" Liliana asked, staring up at him. "Won't you join us?"

"I suppose I could," Hopkins said, settling to his knees and reaching over to snag a bit of jerky, while using his other hand to keep Mollie away from the food. "I do have to deliver a message, though. Lady Rendon wants to speak with you." His eyes connected with Caspian's and there was something in them that Caspian didn't like.

What was wrong? His heart sank. He didn't want to leave Liliana and Sophia, but his mother had called, and he needed to answer.

On the plus side, he could avoid sharing his food with a goat now.

"I'll be back as soon as I can be," he said to both girls, getting to his feet. "Hopkins, take care of the ladies for me."

"Of course," Hopkins said, turning to Liliana with a smile. "So why are we having a tea party with a baby goat?"

Caspian made his way into the manor and went up the stairs to his mother's parlor. He let himself in and sat down across from her.

Why did it feel like she was about to court-martial him?

His mother looked up from her embroidery and pinned him with a stare. "I heard that you've been romancing the goat girl."

Caspian sighed. Of course it was this. No small talk first, just getting right into it? "I have been," he said. "I think I might be falling for her."

"You know, my darling, there is nothing I want more than to see you happily married. But I do want you to consider what your life would be like if you give up on finding a lord's daughter to marry. Can you provide for her? Will you have to find a position in some other lord's manor? Would you consider staying here and being on the payroll as a guard? Would you be happy not running a manor like we've raised you to do? Would she be content with her husband being in a more dangerous profession?"

Caspian let his mother stop asking questions before nodding slowly. "I've been thinking about it. Obviously, I'm not going to rush into things. But yes, I do believe I could be a guard, and I do believe she would be worth it. I can't imagine leaving her to go find another lady and I can't picture myself with anyone but her."

He stood and began pacing the room, unable to contain his nervous energy anymore. "You don't know her, Mother, but I've gotten to know her pretty well since I came home, and she's wonderful. She loves with her whole heart, and she's so sweet and kind, and even though no one in the manor is overly friendly with her she has made amazing friends in the town and they all talk about how wonderful she is. And she's so sweet with the goats. You know I don't even like animals," he admitted, and his mother laughed. "But I've been spending time with them because that's how to spend time with her and I have to admit, they're kind of growing on me."

His mother's eyes widened. "Really?"

He grinned. "Yeah. I do believe that," he said slowly, "I could be convinced that goats are not all that bad."

Lady Rendon laughed. "I suppose your sister would be very happy to hear that. She does think quite highly of her."

"You asked Liliana about her?" Caspian asked, raising an eyebrow.

His mother colored slightly. "I might have," she admitted. "I don't think she realized why, but when I heard that you'd been spending a lot of time with Sophia, I wanted to know more about her."

"I think you would like her," he told her with a smile on his face. "She reminds me a lot of you, always looking out for something to do that would help somebody else. And you know, she makes really good butter," he added with a grin. "It's the most delicious thing I've ever had on bread."

His mother smiled. "Darling, you know I wish we could set you up with an estate of your own."

He shook his head. "I know this is how it works. And I'll be honest—as much as I would love running an estate of my own someday, I can't see anything but her now."

Lady Rendon reached out her hand and he walked over and took it. "That makes me happy, Caspian. And you understand you would have to work in someone else's household for the rest of your life, or start a trade, or do something else?"

"I don't mind being a guard. I'm good at it," Caspian said with a grin. "Even if I wish it was a cleaner job."

His mother laughed. "You're so funny. You and your brothers got so dirty as children. I don't know how you turned out to be so concerned about cleanliness."

Caspian settled back into his chair and shrugged. "I don't know, maybe it was the time my oldest brother dumped me in a mud puddle, and we had to walk back home for hours. The mud caked onto my skin and dried and I never thought I would be rid of the feeling."

His mother laughed again. "I suppose that might do it. It makes me happy to think that you're growing up, even if my heart doesn't want to think you're not my little boy anymore."

"I thought you said I'll always be your little boy?" he asked, glancing down at the plate of food he'd been carefully avoiding looking at since he walked into the room.

Lady Rendon smiled. "That's true. And as long as cookies are involved, I believe you'll always be a little boy. Go ahead, dear, you can eat one."

Caspian grinned. "You do know the way to my heart, Mother."

He was reaching to pick up a cookie when he heard a loud gasp from the other side of the door.

The voice sounded familiar, and his heart sank.

His mother turned and frowned. "Who was that?"

"It sounded like Sophia," he said grimly.

"You better go find out," his mother said, but he was already on his way to the door.

As he opened it, he caught a glimpse of Sophia turning the corner, making no noise as she tiptoed away.

"Sophia," he called, and she broke into a run.

Of course.

He turned back to his mother, who simply nodded her head and said, "Go."

So he ran.

CHAPTER THIRTEEN
SOPHIA

SOPHIA'S HEART WAS TRYING to beat its way out of her chest as she ran down the hallway and down the stairs toward the kitchen.

How could she have been so stupid?

She should have known Caspian wasn't a normal guard.

How could she have ignored the signs for so long?

He hadn't acted normally from the beginning. He hadn't attended a single evening meal in the servants' dining hall, for heaven's sake. She should have known that something was different about him.

She'd been escorting Liliana back to the family's wing and on her way back to the courtyard had heard his voice.

She didn't mean to eavesdrop, but she couldn't help hearing what he was saying.

When she'd overheard him calling Lady Rendon his mother, it felt like he'd stabbed her with a knife.

All this time, he'd been keeping a huge secret from her.

It was probably better that she found out now...but she felt betrayed.

Why had no one else said anything?

Liliana hadn't ever said a word about him being her brother. She'd just assumed he was the guard assigned to follow Liliana when she went on adventures with Sophia.

Dietrich had been right to warn her away, even if he hadn't known exactly what was wrong. Because he would have warned her if he knew that Caspian was nobility.

Right?

She could hear Caspian's footsteps thudding on the floor behind her as she darted into the kitchen and hid around the back of the door.

Maybe no one had noticed her. They seemed particularly inclined to ignore her anyway—what would make today any different?

Caspian crashed through the kitchen door and slammed to a stop. "Where's Sophia?" he demanded.

Sophia watched with wide eyes as no one said anything, even though half of the kitchen could clearly see her hiding behind the door.

"I know she came in here. Where is she?" Caspian said.

Cook's eyes shifted to Sophia for barely half a second, but it was long enough for Caspian to realize where she was. He moved the door, and his brown eyes took her in. Could he tell that she was shaking?

"Sophia," he said softly. "What's wrong?"

She shook her head. She didn't want to talk to him.

"Tell me what happened," he said.

"Why don't you tell me, Lord Rendon?" she asked quietly, though the words had a bite to them.

His eyes widened. "You didn't know."

It wasn't a question.

She didn't want to hear his excuses. He'd known who he was all this time, and he hadn't told her. That wasn't something you should keep from someone, especially if you were spending time with them.

Maybe she'd been reading it wrong. Maybe he wasn't trying to get to know her like she thought. Maybe that was simply her inexperience talking. Maybe he only saw her as a friend.

But even a friend should know who you were.

Did everyone at the café know who he was? Had they kept silent, too?

"Sophia, please." He offered his hand. "Let me explain."

There was a lump in her throat as she swallowed, unsure of what to say. Everyone in the kitchen was staring at her, which was the most attention they'd paid to her since she'd arrived. She felt like she was naked under their gaze, and she knew they would be talking about this for weeks to come.

They'd probably already been talking about her for weeks, ever since he started spending time with her.

Come to think of it, the girls in her room had been awfully quiet the past few weeks. She should have known then that something was wrong. She'd heard them gossiping before—the lack of it should have been a sign.

Now she knew. She hadn't heard it because the current gossip was about her.

"Please," he said again in barely a whisper.

The outer door opened, and a stable hand came racing in. "Where's Sophia? Her dang goats are out again."

Sophia's eyes widened and she scrambled around Caspian and raced for the outer door.

Of course they'd gotten out right now. Why not? One more thing for her to worry about.

If Ivy got out of the courtyard, chasing her would be awful, and she did not want to deal with that right now.

It wasn't until she was halfway to the barn that she realized Caspian was keeping pace with her. "Let me help," he said.

She ignored him and grabbed the leads off the wall of the barn. One of the stable hands pointed to the main door and she ran, hoping the guards had prevented the goats from running out the front gate.

Thankfully, they were still in the main courtyard, but it looked like Ivy was in a fine mood as she ran and avoided the two stable hands who were chasing her.

Sophia hurried toward Ivy. She gestured for the stable hands to herd her toward the outer pen. If Sophia could get her pinned against a fence, it would be much easier to catch her.

It took forever, but she finally pinned Ivy against a fence with the help of the two stable hands and wrapped the lead rope around her neck.

One down. Two to go.

She handed the lead rope off to a stable hand and grabbed the other one she'd looped around her shoulders, preparing to go find Valley or Meadow, when she noticed Caspian already had both. He had a lead rope around Valley's neck and was holding Meadow by the neck with his bare hand.

He was actually touching a goat?

If Sophia hadn't been mad at him, she would have been impressed.

All three adults were accounted for. Hopkins and a stable hand were holding the twins, and Terra was settled into a nook near the barn, nodding off despite the chaos.

Where was Mollie?

"I'm so sorry, Sophia," Hopkins said, approaching her with Ned in his arms. The baby goat struggled to get down, but he held tightly. "I was trying to put Mollie back and they all bolted out the gate."

"Where's Mollie?" she asked, looking around wildly.

She couldn't lose her favorite.

What if she'd jumped into the well? Or snuck out of the courtyard in the hubbub? Sophia scanned the whole courtyard and then looked toward the barn, her jaw dropping when she noticed a brown baby goat dancing along the top of the barn.

"How did she even get up there?" she asked as she made her way to Caspian and looped the extra lead around Meadow's neck.

Caspian let out a laugh. "Of course she's on top of the barn. Why is she your favorite?"

Sophia rolled her eyes. "I don't know. At this point, she's not going to be my favorite anymore."

"I'll get her," Caspian said, handing her the lead rope for Meadow.

Sophia had forgotten she was mad at him until his hand brushed against hers and a hot wave of emotion swept through her.

She didn't want his help.

"I'll get her. The goats are my job, Lord Caspian."

He turned to her, heat flaring in his eyes. "Don't call me that," he said. "That's not what I want you to call me."

"It's the truth, though, isn't it?" She hated the way her voice broke. "And you didn't tell me. You lied to me."

Caspian shook his head, reaching for her, but he dropped his hands before touching her. "I never meant to lie to you, Sophia. I had no idea that you didn't know."

"Why should I believe that?" Sophia said, her voice breaking again.

Caspian laughed, even though it wasn't funny. "Honestly," he said, "I don't really believe it myself. I just assumed that someone would have told you who I was. I assumed that someone would have mentioned I was coming home, or even mentioned that Liliana's brother had just arrived. I never for an instant thought that you didn't know who I was, and I am so sorry that you had to find out this way, because I never meant to keep my identity a secret." His voice cracked as he added, "Please believe me."

Sophia sniffed as tears threatened to fall. "I can't believe that you were Lord Rendon's son this whole time," she said, "and nobody thought I should know."

Caspian took a step closer, though there wasn't much space between them to begin with. "I'm sorry," he said softly. "I wish you had known."

"Why?" she asked, and it felt like the answer would change everything.

"I'm sure feeling like I kept this secret from you must hurt more than I know. I would never want to hurt you, and I'm sorry that it took so long for the truth to come out, because I'm falling in love with you, Sophia. I started falling a long time ago, and I don't know what I'll do if you can't forgive me for this."

Sophia swallowed.

He was falling in love with her?

She turned away from him to collect her thoughts. She looked up at the top of the barn, where Mollie was still prancing and jumping. "Let's save the baby goat," she said, her voice sounding funny to her own ears. "Liliana will never forgive me if Mollie gets hurt."

Caspian waited a moment before nodding and hurrying away.

Sophia watched him go, clutching the lead ropes in her hand, before nudging Valley and Meadow to get them walking back to the barn.

She could let him save Mollie while she decided if she wanted to speak to him ever again.

She wanted to believe him. She wanted to believe that he wouldn't purposely keep his identity from her, and she wanted to believe that he hadn't known. But it still felt like he'd been keeping it from her, and she didn't know how to reconcile that deception with the Caspian that she knew...and was falling in love with.

It didn't make sense, but neither did her feelings.

Maybe this was just part of loving someone.

But could you really love someone and keep that kind of information a secret? Did he really love her?

Her heart ached, and she didn't know what to think as she put Valley and Meadow back in their stall with Ivy and the babies.

She returned to the courtyard to watch Caspian. He was scaling the side of the barn, climbing up the lower outer buildings that Mollie must have climbed up.

How the baby goat had managed to do it, Sophia wasn't sure. But then again, baby goats often defied the laws of nature in the ways they managed to get into things.

Her heart was in her throat as Caspian reached the roof of the barn and began crawling across it slowly. If he spooked Mollie and she fell...or if Caspian fell...Sophia didn't want to think about it.

They should have sent one of the other guards or a stable hand up there. Someone less important than Lord Rendon's son.

But she knew that he was doing it for her, even though he didn't like the goats.

Her heart softened at the thought, but was rescuing a baby goat enough to make up for weeks of lying to her about his identity?

Sophia remembered the way Cook hadn't argued when Caspian said he was taking her into town and her cheeks flushed. She should have seen the signs. She should have known. Maybe she really was just that stupid.

The way he hadn't been at meals, the way everyone listened to him, the way he did whatever he wanted and didn't follow any set schedule. The way he was the one managing the Fall Festival. It all made sense now.

And she was the one who hadn't realized any of it.

No wonder everyone hadn't told her. They were probably all laughing at her for being oblivious.

Everyone in the courtyard watched as Caspian made his way toward Mollie. When she noticed him and started to skitter backwards, he slowly settled into a squat on the roof and pulled something out of his pocket, offering it to the baby goat.

Sophia watched in amazement as Mollie picked her way across the roof and began investigating whatever Caspian held in his hand long enough for him to reach out, grab her, and pull her tightly to his chest.

The guards and stable hands whooped and cheered as Caspian slowly made his way back across the roof of the barn. He jumped down to the lean-to against the side, where they kept much of the straw, then jumped down to the stack of hay bales next to it and climbed down.

Sophia hurried across the courtyard, meeting him at the bottom.

He transferred Mollie into her arms, and she pulled the goat into a tight hug. Tears began to drip down her nose onto the baby goat's soft brown fur.

"I promise, I never meant to lead you on," Caspian said softly. "Will you forgive me for not telling you who I was?"

With her heart in her throat, Sophia nodded. Even if she wasn't entirely sure that she could, she owed him at least that much for saving Mollie.

But what happened now?

"I know I can't go back and change what happened," he said, "but I would love to go forward with you knowing who I am, and I would love to get to know you even better. Will you go to the Fall Festival with me?"

Mollie let out a bleat and gave Sophia a tiny head-butt under her chin, giving Sophia a moment to think. She almost didn't trust herself to speak, but she had to ask. "Go with you as a couple?" she asked. "Or go with you, as in, everyone at the manor is going together?"

Caspian chuckled. "With me. As a couple. Or we could just go as friends. Whatever you want. I just want to spend time with you and see the fruits of all the work we put in."

Sophia swallowed hard. "I suppose so," she said after a moment.

Caspian smiled wryly. "That's the best answer I can hope for right now," he said. "I'm sorry that I didn't tell you."

"I've already forgiven you. You don't have to keep apologizing for it."

He shook his head and took a step closer, his gaze dropping to the goat in her arms before coming back to her face. "No, I'm going to keep apologizing for it. I feel like I should have known better."

"I'm the one who should have known better," she said.

Caspian shrugged. "We could debate it, but I'd rather not. As long as you'll go with me tomorrow, I'm happy."

There was a commotion in the courtyard and Sophia looked around Caspian to see Lady Rendon coming up behind him. She was smiling at Sophia, who suddenly felt like she was facing a dragon. Her eyes widened and she felt a chill run down her spine.

This was the lady of the manor, and Caspian's mother.

Why was she coming to talk to her? Was she going to be let go from her position?

Was a potential relationship with the son of the lord and lady considered a liability? She swallowed and licked her lips, which were suddenly completely dry, as Lady Rendon approached.

"Hello, Sophia," she said sweetly. "I've heard quite a lot about you."

Sophia nodded and stared up at Lady Rendon, unable to speak. She clutched Mollie tighter, as if the baby goat was a shield from any potential bad news.

"I was wondering if you were going to the Fall Festival tomorrow," Lady Rendon asked.

"I am," Sophia said, her voice wobbling.

Was that it?

Lady Rendon smiled. "Well, then, I would like to invite you to come and get ready for the festival with me and Liliana tomorrow," she said, "if that's alright with you."

Sophia's eyes widened even further. "Yes, Lady Rendon," she said after a moment. "I don't know exactly what that means, but I would be honored."

Lady Rendon laughed, a laugh that was so similar to Caspian's. "It doesn't mean much," she said. "But if you want one of our ladies' maids to do your hair, we could arrange that, and I have a dress that hasn't fit me for years that I think would look absolutely stunning on you."

Sophia glanced at Caspian, who was smiling at his mother.

This was good, right?

"Thank you, my lady," she said. "That would be wonderful."

Suddenly even more nervous about the festival, Sophia turned to Caspian. "I should get Mollie back to her mother," she said before slipping away as quickly as she could, rubbing Mollie's head.

She hardly knew what to think about everything that had happened in the last fifteen minutes.

How was this her life now?

Chapter Fourteen
CASPIAN

CASPIAN ANXIOUSLY PACED AT the bottom of the stairs, waiting for his mother, sister, and Sophia to arrive, his heart beating faster every moment he waited.

She'd been upstairs for two hours now, preparing for the Fall Festival, and he didn't know what to expect. The anticipation was going to be the death of him.

"We have to leave soon," he said to Kellan, who grinned at him.

"It's fun seeing you so nervous," his brother said, shoving his shoulder. "You're normally so unflappable."

He glanced at Kellan with a frown. "What do you mean?"

His brother shrugged. "Usually you're the most put together of the three of us. You're always so on top of everything. It's fun to watch you feel like you don't have everything together." He clapped Caspian on the shoulder. "Don't worry. I'm sure you'll figure it all out again soon."

Kellan thought he was the one who had his life together?

That was news to him.

Caspian grimaced. "I sure hope so. I don't know if I will, though. This has me all turned upside down and inside out and I don't know what I'm doing anymore."

"Well, you're still doing better than Gideon," Kellan said.

"Gone again?" Caspian asked quietly.

"Yes. Mother's going to be upset," Kellan said, clenching his jaw. "I don't understand it."

Caspian didn't, either, but Gideon's disappearances had been happening more and more often. Whatever the reason, his brother's situation was getting worse, and they needed to figure it out.

A door opened upstairs, and they turned to watch the stairs. Lord Rendon slipped out of his study and joined them.

Caspian could hear his heartbeat as they heard footsteps coming toward them.

He'd barely seen Sophia since yesterday when she found out that he was actually Lord Caspian Rendon. Even now, a full twenty-four hours later, it still seemed unbelievable to him that she hadn't known who he was.

She had to know he hadn't kept his identity secret on purpose.

He would never lie to her like that.

Liliana appeared at the top of the stairs, smiling the biggest grin Caspian had ever seen on her face. Her long golden hair was done up and she was wearing a beautiful, pale pink dress. She swished her skirts back and forth as she descended the staircase.

Surely this wasn't his baby sister?

His whole world had changed eight years ago when a tiny pink bundle had been placed into his arms.

Apparently, it was going to change again.

She was growing up, and he'd missed the past two years of it.

There was a lump in his throat as his sister reached the bottom of the stairs, her gaze flitting between the three men waiting.

"Do you like it?" she asked shyly, looking down at her dress.

"Absolutely," their father said, and Liliana threw herself at him for a hug. "The most beautiful girl I've ever seen."

"I agree," Caspian said as she made her way to him. He leaned over and gave her a kiss on the top of her head.

"Absolutely gorgeous," their eldest brother said, reaching over to offer his arm. He would be escorting Liliana to the festival.

More footsteps. They all looked up as Lady Rendon appeared at the head of the stairs wearing a dark green dress. Lord Rendon stared at his wife with such pride and love, it made Caspian almost embarrassed. "There's my beautiful bride," his father said with delight. "The most beautiful woman I've ever seen."

Lady Rendon glowed with happiness as she descended the stairs to her husband, who gave her a kiss when she reached him.

A very long and improper kiss.

Too long and too improper.

Caspian turned away after a moment to give them some privacy before he died of embarrassment.

But then there was another set of footsteps and Caspian turned to see Sophia begin to descend the stairs.

His heart stopped beating for a moment.

She was a vision.

She wore a gorgeous dark red dress, almost crimson, which set off her long, dark hair. It had been arranged in an elegant hairstyle, similar to the ones he'd seen on debutantes and noble ladies in Riyel.

But she was more beautiful than any debutante he'd ever seen.

His jaw dropped and he couldn't quite manage to pick it back up. He was sure his family was staring at him, but he couldn't be bothered. He sprang up the staircase and met her halfway, unable to wait for her to reach the bottom.

"You look stunning," he said as he offered his arm and was rewarded with a smile as bright as the sun.

"Thank you," she said. "I feel beautiful."

The dress looked like it had been made for her. Had this really been his mother's dress? There wouldn't have been time for his mother to make something, so it must have been, even if it looked like it was custom-made for Sophia.

Sophia blushed as they descended the remainder of the stairs and were surrounded by his family. "Thank you," she said to Lady Rendon. "This dress is the most beautiful thing I've ever worn. This evening has been wonderful, and we haven't even made it to the festival yet."

His mother laughed. "I am so glad that dress gets to be worn again. I haven't been able to wear it since Liliana was born, but I always loved that one."

"This new dress suits you just as well," Lord Rendon said in a quiet voice as he swept Lady Rendon toward the courtyard.

Caspian took advantage of the opportunity to touch Sophia's hand as he helped her into the carriage, relishing the touch of her fingers against his. He mounted his horse and rode alongside the carriage as they made their way to town.

Every time he glanced inside the carriage, he noticed Sophia smoothing down the fabric of her skirts with a small smile on her face.

She looked like she was made to wear a dress like that.

She looked like she was meant to be the wife of a lord's son.

They pulled up to the edge of the town square and the men dismounted, standing at the ready to help the ladies.

Liliana descended from the carriage first, and Kellan took her hand. Then it was Lady Rendon's turn, and Lord Rendon swooped her away.

Then his Sophia.

Caspian offered his arm, feeling like the luckiest fellow in the world when she took it. "Shall we go see everything we accomplished?" he asked Sophia as they made their way into the center of town.

"I can't wait," Sophia said with a smile.

The glow of the bonfire and the scent of woodsmoke and hot apple cider filled the air. The town square was full of people, all wearing their best clothes. The music was loud and there were already several people dancing near the musicians, while children chased each other through the crowd and adults mingled with food and drink in their hands.

It was perfect.

Satisfaction filled Caspian as he glanced around the square.

They'd pulled it off.

"Would you like some cider?" Caspian asked Sophia. He was leading her toward Thea's booth, already knowing what her answer would be.

The café owner was wearing the dark green apron he suspected was her favorite, given how often she wore it, over what was probably her finest dress.

"Absolutely! I love cider," Sophia said as Thea handed them both a mug, staring suspiciously between the two of them. Was she wondering what to say?

"The festival came together well," Thea said to Caspian after a moment. "Good job."

That wasn't what he'd expected, but he would take it.

Caspian smiled. "Thank you. I had a great helper."

Thea turned to Sophia and smiled. "You look beautiful, dear."

"Thank you," Sophia said, blushing and settling into a tiny curtsy. "Lady Rendon offered to let me borrow this dress."

Speaking of Lady Rendon...Caspian looked at Thea. "Do you know who I am?" he asked.

"I didn't at first," Thea said, "but of course I figured it out quickly."

He took a deep breath and looked down at Sophia. She let out a breath and chewed on her bottom lip.

"You didn't know?" Thea asked Sophia, her eyes widening. "Oh, Sophia, I had no idea that you didn't know."

Sophia sighed. "Apparently everyone thought the same thing."

"Everyone thought the same what?" Dietrich asked, coming around the side of the booth with a tray full of clean mugs.

"Do you know who Caspian is?" Sophia demanded.

Dietrich stared at him, his eyes narrowing. "No?"

"He's Lord Rendon's son," Thea said. "How did you not know that? Did you not listen to Eugenia at all?"

Dietrich set the tray down on the table and raised his hands in innocence. "I don't make a habit of listening to Eugenia's ramblings and gossip."

Thea sighed. "Well, at least you weren't the only one who didn't know, Sophia."

Sophia grumbled, "At least I'm not the only idiot, you mean?"

"Hey now," Dietrich said, "I take offense to that for both of us."

"You're not an idiot," Caspian said, bringing his hand to rest on Sophia's lower back. "You had no way of knowing if no one told you or addressed me by my title in front of you. I'm only sorry that I didn't say it."

"Well, I'm still sorry that I didn't mention it myself," Thea said.

Lord Rendon bumped into Caspian's shoulder. "You're causing a line, son. Also, I would love two cups of cider, Thea."

"Of course, sir," she said with a smile as Dietrich poured a steaming hot mug and handed it to Lord Rendon.

In return, Caspian handed over a generous number of coins and Thea's eyes brightened. "Thank you."

"Have a great festival," Caspian said, putting gentle pressure on Sophia's back to guide her away from the booth.

His father followed them to where Lady Rendon and Liliana stood waiting. "You did a wonderful job with the festival, my darling," Lady Rendon said as her husband handed her the steaming mug. "I couldn't have done a better job myself."

"Oh, I'm sure you could have," Caspian said with a grin. "But I'm glad it meets your approval."

"We must find Beatrice and tell her how happy we are," Lady Rendon told Lord Rendon. "You know it means a great deal to her."

"And she did the vast majority of the work," Caspian said.

"Come, let's walk." Lord Rendon offered an arm to his wife. "We'll see if we can find her."

"Shall we walk with them, or make our own journey?" Caspian asked Sophia.

"I would love to stop at our booth and make sure my soaps are organized well," Sophia said. "I was so busy with your mother this afternoon, I didn't get to come and make sure it was all arranged to my satisfaction."

"Does it matter how they're arranged?" Caspian raised an eyebrow.

"Absolutely," Sophia said. "Trust me."

He laughed as they made their way to the manor's booth. There was a table filled with honey from their bees, Sophia's goat milk soap, and baskets that had been made during the last winter. Sophia pulled away from him to arrange her soaps neatly, the kitchen staff member minding the booth smiling at her indulgently as she did so.

"That's enough," he said, attempting to take her hand after she'd touched every single piece at least once.

"Hold on, I have to get the soap off my fingers," she said. "I wouldn't want to get it on this fine dress."

He offered his arm, clad in a coat. "Wipe it off on me."

"It will get it dirty," she protested.

"It's soap. It'll wash."

She frowned at him but wiped her hand on his sleeve, leaving behind a tiny streak of soap.

"Now I smell wonderful," he said to her. The words made her laugh, and his whole night got better just for hearing it.

"Now, that's enough time spent with soap," he said, taking her hand and pulling her toward the bonfire. "We have an evening to enjoy."

The glow of the bonfire made Sophia come alive as she tapped her feet to the lively tune being played by the townsfolk. He wrapped his arm around her waist and pulled her closer as they sipped their hot cider around a roaring bonfire.

Could it get any better than this?

Actually, it could, and he knew just how to do it.

He reached out and took Sophia's drink from her, putting them down on a stump, before holding out a hand. "May I have this dance, miss?"

He was rewarded with a bright smile and her hand slipping into his. "Of course," she said, "though I will warn you, I don't know how to dance."

"I can teach you."

He attempted to spin her into his arms, and she landed on his toes.

"Are you sure?" she asked, grimacing as she clutched at his coat and stepped backward.

"I'm sure," he said. She was light as a feather, and he'd barely felt her stomping on his foot.

"There's a reason I spend most of my time with goats." Sophia laughed as he pulled her in close again. The light of the fire danced in her eyes as he attempted to teach her a few basic steps, most of them ending with her on top of his toes.

It was a good thing he'd worn his boots.

It didn't matter though.

She was beautiful.

She was his.

He was getting ahead of himself, maybe, but it certainly seemed like Sophia was happy with him, too.

They could make this work, because he could do this for the rest of his life—and judging by the way his parents were smiling as they watched, it wouldn't be hard to convince them that he'd found the one.

After several songs, the music slowed, and Caspian pulled Sophia close for a waltz. "I've never done this before," Sophia said, tilting her neck to look up at him. He didn't often regret how tall he was, but the way it made her look up so far couldn't be comfortable. But she did it anyway, smiling up at him as she let him twirl her around.

This was everything he'd ever dreamed of.

And now that it was happening, he couldn't believe it.

"I think it was a success," Sophia said, looking around with a smile at the townsfolk and nobility mingling around the bonfire. All four noble families in the Northlands region were represented tonight, even if only by one person, and it seemed like the whole town was there. "You did a wonderful job."

"Thank you for all your help," he said.

Sophia laughed. "I did nothing. You were the one who took this responsibility and made it a success, and I'm very proud of you."

Warmth spread through his chest at her words. Somehow she knew exactly what to say. "Thank you," he said softly. He stopped dancing and cupped her cheek in his hand. She leaned into his touch, closing her eyes,

He leaned down and gently pressed his lips to hers. Sparks from the fire flew higher and brighter and it felt like his world was exploding into flames along with it as everything faded but the two of them and they were alone in their own world.

Just him and Sophia and the feelings between them.

She was the one.

He had to tell her.

He caressed her cheek and pulled away, looking down at her with a smile.

She smiled up at him, her eyes gleaming in the night, and she rested her head against his chest.

This evening was perfect. It was official. Nothing could make it any better.

He pulled her away from the dancing, glancing around for their drinks, but they were long gone. He found a log near the fire to sit on and pulled her close, wrapping his arm around her shoulders.

She leaned into him, and he rested his head against her hair, rubbing her shoulder as they enjoyed the warmth of the fire.

Dietrich walked past with a tray of hot chocolate. Caspian flagged him down and handed him a coin in exchange for two mugs, handing one to Sophia. She accepted it happily, burrowing into his side as she wrapped her hands around the mug.

He'd never felt more alive.

But it wasn't long before one of the lord's sons that he'd grown up with recognized him and hurried over.

Not that he had anything against Percival, but he didn't want to talk to him right now.

He exchanged pleasantries, hoping to make it a quick conversation, but then Percival asked about his two years in Riyel. After a few minutes, Sophia pulled away from him and patted him on the shoulder before wandering away.

He didn't blame her. She probably didn't want to hear talk about Riyel after she'd been forced away from it. She had friends here in town—he couldn't monopolize her for the entire evening, even if he wanted to.

But when he finally got away from Percival and went to look for her again, he couldn't find her.

He scanned the crowd, looking for any sign of her, but she seemed to be gone.

He walked the entire way around the bonfire, checked in all the booths, including under the table of the manor's booths, and still couldn't find her.

Where was she?

Had she decided to go home?

He made his way to Thea's booth and asked her, "Have you seen Sophia?"

Thea shook her head. "No, but she may have decided to head home early if she was getting overwhelmed. It wouldn't surprise me at all. She's been known to slip out of the café if things get too chaotic for her."

Caspian stuffed down the twinge of disappointment that tried to float to the surface. Sophia leaving early wouldn't put a damper on how wonderful this evening had been.

He would treasure this memory for the rest of his life.

"I just wish she had told me," he said. "I would have escorted her home.

Thea shrugged and turned to help another customer. "She probably didn't want to interrupt you," she said. "Go enjoy the festival."

Caspian listened to Thea but continued to look out for Sophia just in case.

He didn't want the night to end, but he wished he could end it with Sophia.

Chapter Fifteen
Sophia

Sophia had tried to listen to Caspian talk to Percival, but as he began telling stories of his life in Riyel, fear flooded her body. Talk of Riyel made her anxious and sad, as her mind brought up images of her previous life. Evenings spent in a dark room in the basement, days without speaking to anyone, and more than a few nights with an empty belly.

She didn't want to think about it.

The Fall Festival had been nothing short of magical, from the moment she'd begun getting ready with Liliana and Lady Rendon, to spending the evening with Caspian, dancing in his arms, and having her first kiss under the stars next to a bonfire.

It had been everything she ever imagined and more.

So she didn't want to ruin that by sitting there, listening to talk of Riyel, and remembering how horrible her life had been.

She'd pulled her arm out from Caspian's and patted his shoulder to let him know that she was leaving before she wandered off. She wanted to talk to Thea and ask what she thought about her and Caspian...and she wanted to see how many of her soaps had sold.

As she made her way toward the manor's booth, she ran into multiple people, but only one of them grabbed her arm and pulled her to a stop.

"Hello, young lady," a scratchy voice said as an old woman with a hood over her head and a stooped back pulled her to the side. "You are the most stunning young lady at this festival. I would be honored if you would care to feast upon an apple from my tree."

Sophia shook her head. "Oh, thank you, but I'm not hungry."

The old woman grabbed her arm tighter. "I would be honored if you would spread the word about how delicious my apples are."

Sophia glanced around for anyone else, but there was no one near in the darkness away from the fire.

The old woman produced a green apple from the folds of her cloak.

"Oh, I'm sorry," Sophia said. "I don't like green apples—I only like red ones."

The woman snarled. "I should have known you'd be problematic."

Sophia tried to pull away, yanking her arm, and the movement made the woman's hood fall back.

It was Lady Manning.

Sophia stumbled back.

No.

Not her.

Not here.

She tried to scream but an arm came around her and covered her mouth.

She was carried away into the night. She kicked and flailed, but it was no use. She might be stronger now than when she'd run away, but she wasn't strong enough against the man holding her.

She couldn't even get a scream out with how tightly his hand covered her face.

He carried her far enough away that no one would be able to hear her screams, the happy sounds of celebration long faded into the night, before dumping her onto a hay-filled wagon. He tied her hands and feet and put a gag in her mouth for good measure.

Lady Manning watched in triumph before climbing into her own carriage.

As the wagon started into motion and she fell onto her side, Sophia wanted to burst into tears.

It had finally happened.

Lady Manning had caught up to her.

What was she going to do with her?

What was the point of coming for her?

Lady Manning didn't need more servants in Riyel.

No, the fate coming for her was likely worse than that.

What would Caspian think when he couldn't find her?

Tears pricked at her eyes.

Would he come for her?

Would he even notice she was gone?

Would he think she'd abandoned him?

Sophia prayed he would not think she'd left him.

She prayed Caspian would come for her, that he would find her and save her before it was too late, before Lady Manning's plans would come to fruition.

Tears rolled down her cheeks and she hid her face in the scratchy hay in the bottom of the wagon.

How had Lady Manning found her? And why? Why couldn't she just let her run away? Why couldn't she just let it be? Why did she feel the need to track her down and bring her back? If she was going to kill her, why couldn't she have just killed her there? Did she need the theatrics of bringing Sophia home to kill her?

No.

Lady Manning's household and Riyel were not home anymore.

Home was the manor with her goats.

Oh, her goats! What would they do without her? Would the stable master send them away since he had no patience for them? Would Liliana be heartbroken? Would Mollie miss her?

Sophia stifled the sob that threatened to break out through the gag.

Caspian would find out she was missing, and he would catch up to her.

He had to come for her.

The wagon jostled and she fell awkwardly onto her stomach, landing on her bound hands. Pain ran up her arm.

She just wanted to be home.

Home, in the Northlands, with Caspian and his family and her friends.

Maybe Thea would notice she was gone. Or Dietrich. Any of the others.

If only one of them would notice she'd left the festival—all it would take was one.

Caspian was a guard. Surely he would come look for her. She couldn't imagine Caspian ignoring the fact that a woman of his acquaintance had disappeared, no matter who the woman was—and after everything that had happened this evening, she had to assume he'd be even more inclined to look for her.

The need to be back by the bonfire with his arm around her hit like a bale of hay. She could no longer smell the smoke of the bonfire and the fact that she couldn't even smell her home anymore made her want to cry more.

She just wanted to sleep, to fall into ignorant slumber, but she couldn't imagine falling asleep now.

She hadn't recognized the man binding her.

Was he Lady Manning's new henchman? He must be loyal to her in order to kidnap an innocent girl on her orders.

She wanted to know, and yet, the knowledge wouldn't change anything. It wouldn't make her feel any better. Maybe she should just pretend that they were taking her away to kill her. That might make anything else seem better in comparison.

Anything else and there was a chance Caspian would come and save her, or that she would be able to run away again.

No. Lady Manning would never allow her to run away again.

She knew that much.

Time seemed to stretch forever and yet not long enough as the wagon continued to roll on through the darkness, with only a few torches and the moon lighting their path. Sophia began to grow cold. The fine dress from Lady Rendon was not meant for staying warm on a chilly night.

She welcomed the cold, though. It reminded her of her first escape from Lady Manning's clutches.

She'd done it once. She could do it again.

She was stronger now, stronger than she'd ever known.

And this time, she could run straight to Caspian.

"Huntsman," Lady Manning screeched. "We will stop here for the night and tomorrow we will continue on our way. I can't sleep with this incessant jolting."

The wagon ground to a halt with a whine and she pretended she wasn't awake. If she didn't move a muscle, maybe they would leave her alone.

"Set up camp," a masculine voice ordered from somewhere behind her.

Was it the person who had grabbed her? He wasn't the old captain of the guard. He would never have tied Sophia up.

As she listened to the guards around her setting up a camp, Sophia tried to take deep breaths. She was far too outnumbered to run for it right now, even if her legs were free.

The idea of sleeping and being unaware of what was going on made her stomach turn, but she would need to be well rested in order to make her escape.

Sophia closed her eyes, praying Caspian would come and find her, or she would have the opportunity to escape herself.

Because she knew once she was back in Lady Manning's home, there would be no chance.

It was light when she awoke. She shivered in the cold of early morning, Lady Rendon's dress a flimsy barrier against the dew and the cool breeze.

How she longed for her cozy bed at home, with plenty of quilts and blankets, and a roaring fire in the kitchen.

She took a deep breath as the reality of her situation crashed into her awareness once again. The blissful avoidance of sleep fell away, and her heart began to beat faster.

Lady Manning was bringing her back to Riyel.

And if she made it there, she wouldn't make it back out again.

Somehow she knew that, deep in her bones.

She had to get away before they got into the city.

She prayed that Caspian would come for her. Surely he had realized by now that she was missing. The ride to Riyel took time—she should know. She'd walked it on her way to the Northlands almost a year ago. Her mind strayed to the several days she'd been walking before Dietrich had found her, the freezing wind and snow biting through her worn clothing and her body shaking from the chills. She hadn't eaten in several days, and getting water to drink from the creek only made the cold worse.

If Dietrich hadn't found her, she wasn't sure she would have survived.

But he had found her and brought her to Thea. They had placed her before a roaring fire, clothed her, fed her, given her hot cider to warm her. Thea had found her a place to sleep that night, and in the morning sent Dietrich to Lord Rendon to ask if he had any openings for a maid.

She didn't know what Dietrich had told Lord Rendon, but she was given a place there, and barely a week later, the manor had goats that needed someone to tend to them, and she was given the job.

And then, not too long ago, Caspian had arrived, and her life had changed.

She didn't want to do life without him.

He had to come for her.

He had time to get to her. One man on horseback was faster than a wagon and a carriage. She didn't know how long the drive normally took, but it had to be at least another day.

He could catch up to them.

Though maybe she shouldn't wish for him to come. She had no idea how many guards there were, and as much as she knew her fate would be difficult, it would be better than watching Caspian die. And Lady Manning would make sure she saw it, if she got an inkling of how much Caspian meant to her.

Sophia didn't like thinking of all the things she'd been forced to do, but she knew beyond a doubt Lady Manning would make her watch them hurt Caspian.

Maybe it would be better if he didn't come. It would probably be better for him. But she knew, without a doubt, that Caspian was not the kind of man who could walk away and not follow her.

Her traitorous heart couldn't wait for him to arrive.

"We need to leave," Lady Manning screeched, her voice closer than Sophia had been expecting, and she flinched.

Had Lady Manning seen that she was awake? Would she say something to Sophia?

"I have plans for you," Lady Manning's voice rasped uncomfortably close to Sophia's head. "You should never have run away. But I've found you, and you will never get away again."

She let out a cackle as she walked away, and Sophia began trembling.

She didn't have to imagine what sort of plans they might be. She'd had a taste of it before. It was never pleasant, and often included a lack of food and water.

But she'd survived it before. She could survive it again. And Caspian would come for her.

Sophia took a deep breath.

Caspian was a man of honor. He wouldn't care for someone and allow them to disappear without trying to find out why. And he wouldn't have kissed her if he didn't care for her.

No, he had to know something was wrong. Especially since he knew she was potentially still in danger from Lady Manning. He had enough pieces of the puzzle—hopefully he would be able to put them together quickly enough.

The wagon jolted as it started to move forward, and Sophia took a deep breath again...and again...and again.

Caspian would come for her.

He had to.

Because if he didn't, she might not make it out of this alive.

Chapter Sixteen
CASPIAN

Caspian couldn't shake the sense of unease as he sat up in bed.

Something didn't feel right about the way Sophia had disappeared last night.

He still hadn't seen her as he helped his sleeping sister and exhausted mother get into the carriage, and he'd reluctantly followed them home after asking Thea to keep an eye out for Sophia.

But something was wrong. He could feel it.

He quickly got dressed and hurried down to the kitchen. "Have you seen Sophia?" he asked Cook.

She shook her head. "I don't know. Ask her roommates."

"Who are her roommates?" Caspian asked.

"I don't know," Cook said. Caspian fought down his frustration at her unhelpfulness. She was bustling around preparing breakfast for his family. She had no idea what had happened last night.

But he didn't care about breakfast—he cared about Sophia.

He glanced around at the full kitchen and said, very loudly, "Has anyone seen Sophia this morning?"

Everyone in the room paused and looked around at each other before shaking their heads no. Caspian was about to ask who shared a room with her when a voice piped up from the back and said, "She wasn't in our room this morning, either."

Caspian froze. "She never came home?"

"Not unless she slept in the barn with the goats."

That didn't seem likely, but he raced out the outer door toward the barn anyway.

Sophia wasn't with the goats, either.

Caspian swore and called to a stable hand, "Bring my horse," as he ran toward the house to get his coat and sword.

Kellan followed him into the courtyard as Caspian checked his horse's saddle. "Where are you going?"

"Sophia never came home last night," Caspian said shortly as he adjusted the girth. "I should have gone after her last night. I'm going to make sure she's not in town, and then I'm going to look for her."

"She probably just spent the night with a friend," his brother began, but Caspian shook his head.

"She ran away from her old household because the lady was cruel and mistreated her. She knew there was a chance they would come after her. I'm willing to bet that she was taken, and I need to get her back. I should have followed her yesterday, and I didn't, and that's my fault."

Kellan clapped his hand on Caspian's shoulder. "It's not your fault. Let me get some men together."

Caspian shook his head. "I'm not waiting."

Kellan frowned. "We'll catch up."

Caspian nodded. "Don't take long."

Before he could swing up on his horse, Cook hurried out of the kitchen with a bundle of food.

"Are you going after her?" she asked.

Caspian nodded.

"Take this," Cook said. "We hope you find her."

Caspian put the food in his saddlebags, mounted his horse, and rode hard to town.

He came to a stop outside of the café and looped the reins around a post before rushing inside.

Thea looked up at him, and her eyes widened when she saw his face. She shook her head. "She's not here." Fear tinged her voice. "And last night, I remembered that a week or so ago, there was a stranger in town, and she was in the café that day."

Caspian cursed again. "I'm going after her," he said. "If anyone wants to follow, they can. I'm assuming they're taking her to Riyel."

Thea didn't ask questions, but she nodded.

He had to get to Sophia before they got her to the city.

Caspian ran back to his horse, and they flew past the edge of town, headed south. He'd only been riding for a couple of hours when he saw signs of a camp, including still warm embers.

It had to be them. The road to the Northlands wasn't well traveled, and he hadn't noticed any newcomers in town last night or passed anyone on his journey yet.

It was an odd place to stop, though. They'd be to the inn that marked the halfway point long before nightfall.

Unless they rode long past dusk, they'd have to stop another night and he would be able to catch up to them.

The tracks diverged off the main path after the camp and he followed them.

There was no way to know what he was riding toward, but the fire had been large, larger than one would expect for two men, and there were wheel tracks for more than one vehicle.

Had Lady Manning come herself to track down Sophia?

What would have caused Lady Manning to come to find Sophia herself?

There was no reason for a lady to leave her household to chase after a servant who had left. Servants left all the time for whatever reasons they had.

There had to be some deeper meaning for her mistreatment and pursuit of Sophia. But what was the reason? Why was she putting so much energy into one girl?

What did Sophia know that Lady Manning didn't want anyone else to know?

Caspian spurred on his horse. He was a fool. He should have been with her last night, shouldn't have let her out of his sight. She'd told him that she was worried about being found.

He'd promised to protect her.

He'd failed.

What was he doing last night instead of protecting her? Catching up with a childhood friend and ignoring her. How could he have allowed himself to be distracted?

After such a wonderful evening, he'd gotten distracted, and now she was gone.

They must have taken her when she left him, because he'd excused himself to look for her shortly after she wandered away.

If she hadn't left him, if he had been focused only on her, she might still be with him.

This was his fault, and he needed to fix it.

What was she thinking right now? Was she being treated like a prisoner? Was she being forced to walk, or given a horse? Was she being forced to ride with another man? Jealousy churned with the anger in his gut and if he hadn't been so upset, he might have laughed at himself for being jealous over a hypothetical situation.

He needed to find her.

The road stretched long before him, and he couldn't stop thinking about how she must have felt when she realized she'd been found. When she realized she was being taken back to Riyel. When she realized she would be back in Lady Manning's power.

After a few hard hours of riding, the flat land of the Northlands transitioned to more rolling hills, a forest running along the eastern side of the road. He had to be careful here. He didn't want them to see that he was following them.

As he crested a hill, he noticed riders in the distance. He slowed his horse and turned, riding back down the hill. The last thing he needed was for them to notice that they were being pursued.

He made his way to the forest, heading far enough in that he could barely see the road, before riding south again.

He let himself catch up enough to see a carriage, six guards, and a wagon through the trees.

His Sophia was sitting in the wagon, her hands in her lap in a position that made him think she was bound. His heart sank as he watched her, sitting motionless amidst the jostling.

What was going through her mind?

Was she blaming him for not being there?

Did she think that he had abandoned her?

Was she afraid that she was going to die?

He couldn't take on six guards by himself. Not during the day. He had to wait for nightfall and hope they hadn't made it to the city or hope that his brother would catch up to him by then.

As the day wore on and the carriage continued its sedate pace, he followed just out of sight.

Would Kellan make it in time? Would they have seen the signs that he did and followed the tracks as they left the main road?

When they stopped for the evening, he tied his horse to a tree and settled down to wait for nightfall. He felt guilty eating some of the food that Cook had sent, not knowing if Sophia was being fed, but he needed energy to rescue her and ride home through the night.

When would his brother arrive?

Were they even coming? Was he on his own to rescue Sophia?

It didn't matter if he was. He would rescue her no matter what the cost. As a guard, and as the man who loved her, he couldn't live with himself if he didn't.

As dusk fell, he crept closer so he could see what was happening. He watched as Sophia was taken to the edge of the woods and allowed a moment of privacy.

He itched to run to her and steal her back, but there wasn't enough time before she was brought back to the wagon. The guard who had led her to the woods handed her something and she began to eat.

Thank goodness they were giving her food and water.

It would be a long ride home after he rescued her, and they both needed the energy for it. But they had to go all night—they couldn't risk being chased by six guards.

He should have waited for his brother. But if he had, he might not have caught up to them. As it was, he didn't know if his brother would even find them with how far they were off the road. The longer they had ridden, the farther they had strayed, and the ground had grown dry, so they weren't leaving tracks.

It was entirely possible that they wouldn't find them.

Darkness fell and a fire was built, and Sophia sat in her wagon.

He prayed that she knew he was coming for her, that she wasn't scared, that she was waiting for him and not feeling utterly abandoned.

He prayed that he would be able to rescue her, and they would both escape unharmed.

As the guards settled in for the night, with one lone guard standing watch, he began to creep closer, at times dropping down to crawl in the dirt.

If crawling through the grass and dirt didn't prove how much he loved her, he wasn't sure what else he could do.

Rescuing her would be a good start, though.

Chapter Seventeen
SOPHIA

Sophia sat still as a stone, hoping to avoid being noticed. The Huntsman had brought her to the edge of the woods and given her a moment of privacy, before bringing her back to the wagon and tying her hands together. He'd let her sit on the bench across the front before tying the end of the rope to the wagon and handing her a piece of bread and a piece of cheese, one for each hand.

They hadn't forced the gag on her as they'd left the main road behind. They probably thought they were far enough away from the Northlands that it didn't matter anymore.

Her hope of being rescued was rapidly dwindling with every mile put between them and her new home.

Had Caspian noticed she was gone yet?

Thinking about it only brought tears closer to the surface, so she couldn't allow herself to think about it too much.

She also didn't think about the fact that it was cold away from the fire, and Lady Rendon's beautiful dress was ruined and absolutely terrible at keeping her warm.

She'd survived worse.

Instead she thought about all of her favorite things she'd experienced in the Northlands as she ate the dry bread and cheese.

Thea's drinks, love, and the comfort of the café. Snuggling Ginger in her favorite chair. Playing with Mollie. The day Mollie was born, too.

Mollie was the first baby she'd ever delivered, and being there for the moment new life was born was an incredible thing.

Mollie had been cold, too. Sophia had used a towel to dry her off and snuggled her in the kitchen until she warmed up. She'd brought her back to the barn and watched her nurse for the first time, and ever since that day, she'd been in love with her goats.

Would Mollie think that she'd abandoned her?

No. She couldn't think that.

That would definitely bring tears, and she refused to let them see her cry.

Her mind drifted to Caspian and all the happy moments she'd shared with him...but no. Those thoughts were dangerous, too.

She waited for dusk to turn to darkness so she could cry as much as she wanted.

She'd overheard the Huntsman telling Lady Manning they would get to the city by midday tomorrow. Lady Manning had come by the wagon to gloat several times but hadn't said anything of substance that would tell her what she was planning.

All it did was fill her with dread for what was awaiting her in Riyel.

She would never stop fighting to get away.

She hadn't known when she escaped the first time how wonderful life could be. She hadn't known the feeling of a warm animal snuggled in your lap, or the feeling of a friend giving you a hug for no reason, or the feeling of a man holding you close and kissing you like he never wanted to let you go.

Now that she knew life could be like that...she would never stop fighting to get it back.

So she sat and waited and prayed that she would make it out alive, that Caspian would find her, and that they would make it back to the Northlands and safety.

"We'll be home tomorrow," a menacing voice said from behind her.

A chill ran down Sophia's back. She refused to turn to see her. It wouldn't help the situation. Lady Manning didn't like it when Sophia looked into her eyes, so there was no point.

"You are worthless, and the only thing you're good for is serving me," Lady Manning continued.

Sophia's heart lightened at the words. It was the first time Lady Manning had said anything that led her to believe she wouldn't be killed.

"And I can't wait to punish you for having the audacity to run away from me after all these years. I raised you, fed you, clothed you—and you ran away? Such insolence must be punished, don't you agree?"

Sophia's heart was beating faster. Rosaleen was the one who had raised her. Lady Manning had done nothing for her.

"I've had my huntsman searching for you all this time, and now that we've found you, you'll spend the rest of your miserable life serving me and the estate," the woman continued, a sneer in her voice.

Sophia didn't have to turn to know what her face looked like. She knew it all too well—the pursed lips, the haughty eyes, the look of malevolence that never quite disappeared.

"I'll never serve you," Sophia said quietly.

Perhaps it was foolish, but she'd spent her whole life staying silent. She'd never spoken up before, never talked back, never given voice to the words that ran through her head.

"You are cruel and abusive, and though you may keep me imprisoned, you'll never win my spirit."

She turned to face the woman who had made her life a living hell.

Who'd thrown her into a holding cell more than once without reason, forced her to go days without food, and ordered her to do inane tasks for no reason other than spite.

"You finally show some of your father's spirit," the woman said with a haggard laugh. "But it's too late. You are mine, and you will be forever."

Sophia's heart leaped at the mention of her father. Lady Manning had never mentioned him before. Why now?

"Why do you hate me?" she asked. Was it because of her father?

"Don't you wish you knew," Lady Manning said, her lips twisting into the ever-familiar sneer. "As if I'd tell you."

Could she goad her into revealing the truth? Had her apparent meekness and decision to remain calm above all kept her from finding out more information long ago?

"No, I don't suppose you would," Sophia said. "Then I'd have even less reason to be afraid of you."

"You should be afraid," Lady Manning said, her eyes glittering with the hatred that usually simmered under the surface.

"I have no reason to fear you," Sophia said, staring steadily into the face of her captor.

The words rang true for the first time in her life.

She knew what she was worth now.

Nothing that Lady Manning could do would change that.

"You would if you knew the truth," Lady Manning said, her voice growing louder.

"I don't need to know the truth," Sophia bluffed.

She needed to know.

The need burned deep within her.

"As if you never figured out that Lord Manning was your father," Lady Manning said with a sneer. "You don't fool me with your pretend innocence. But you are not worthy of being nobility."

Sophia could barely breathe.

"And if you even think about running away again, maybe I'll forget the law against killing nobility," Lady Manning hissed. "So you remember that."

She turned and stalked away, toward her carriage, and Sophia stared after her.

It couldn't be true. Could it be?

Could she really be Lord Manning's daughter?

Rosaleen had to have known. She'd been serving the Manning family for years before Sophia's birth. Was that why she'd insisted on teaching Sophia how to read and how to talk properly, and told bedtime stories of selfless lords and ladies who always did the right thing?

Sophia stared at the knot tying her to the wagon.

Could she undo it? Whether on purpose or not, her wagon was parked a length away from the carriage and the fire, and she was more isolated than the previous night. It was a better chance than before to escape.

If she was indeed Lord Manning's daughter...she had to get away. She couldn't allow herself to disappear. She couldn't allow Lady Manning to steal her rightful title.

But maybe it was a bluff, a farce, something only intended to intimidate her.

As darkness fell, she looked away from the fire the guards had built far enough away from the wagon that she wouldn't feel even a hint of its warmth. Looking at it was only a reminder of how cold she was.

So she looked away and allowed her eyes to adjust to the darkness, letting a few tears fall. They ran down her cheeks, and she did her best to wipe them with her hands tied.

She couldn't remember what had happened to Lord Manning, and suddenly she desperately wanted to know.

She could vaguely remember a painting of him that hung in the mansion's gallery.

He did have dark hair like she did.

But dark hair was common enough. She couldn't claim he was her father on such a trivial tie.

She had no actual proof of her parentage.

There was a fairly good chance Lady Manning was simply lying to her again to throw her into turmoil. She liked to cause chaos and emotional damage. This could be another example of it.

And yet, it would explain so much of why Sophia was hated above everyone else.

She heard Caspian's voice whispering her name and smothered a laugh.

Wonderful. She was hallucinating now. That would make everything easier to deal with.

Of course, hallucinations might help keep her warmer. Could she hallucinate a fire, too?

"Sophia," she heard again, and her traitorous heart leaped at the sound of his voice.

It wasn't real. It couldn't be real.

But then he was there, behind her, his arms around her, holding her tight, pulling her back against him as he buried his face in her neck and kissed her there. "I'm here," he whispered.

She couldn't see him, but she didn't need to. She knew it was him with every fiber of her being.

"You found me." Tears of relief ran down her face.

She started shaking and couldn't stop it.

"Of course I did," he said, rubbing her arm. "You didn't think I spent two years training to be a guard for no reason, did you? Rescuing beautiful maidens is practically in the job description."

She choked back a laugh. "I was so worried you wouldn't come in time."

"I've been with you since noon," he said. "But I couldn't come until nightfall. Now let's get you out of here." He let go of her for a moment, his hands reappearing with a knife. He cut through the ropes that bound her hands to the wagon, and she turned where she sat and buried her face in his shoulder, her tears instantly creating a wet spot on his shirt.

"Are you hurt?" he asked, his arms coming around her again and oh, it felt so wonderful and so right.

"Only my wrists," she said, sniffling against him. "Let's go, please."

"Of course," he said, pressing a kiss to her hair. But then he muttered a curse. "Guard."

He let go of her and dove underneath the plank she sat on as the guard currently standing watch made his way toward them, Sophia did her best to arrange her skirts to hide Caspian. She moved her hands to the same position they'd been in, grabbing the rope and wrapping it around her wrists, holding the cut end tightly in her fist.

If the guard looked closely, he would notice something was wrong.

Caspian's hand came to rest on her ankle, a reminder that he was with her, and she took a deep breath. She wasn't alone anymore. She could do this.

They just had to get away without all the guards noticing, because there were too many of them for Caspian alone.

The guard made a face at her as he approached.

Sophia's heart beat faster. Was he going to see the rope? Or notice the bulk under her skirts that hadn't been there before?

The guard inspected her face, a mean glint in his eyes, but didn't say or do anything before turning and walking back to the fire.

It was meant purely to intimidate her, and it would have, if she hadn't had Caspian holding on to her like he would never let her go again, his breath warm against her ankle. She didn't notice that she was shaking until Caspian began rubbing the length of her foot, up to her ankle, and back down again. She could feel her foot, in the thin slippers she'd borrowed from Lady Rendon, trembling in his grip.

They certainly weren't the sturdy shoes she usually wore in the barn. She could feel the warmth of his hand through them, which only made her realize how cold her feet were and how desperately she wanted to be warm.

She could be warm when they got home, though.

When the guard had made his way back to the fire and was settled again, Sophia reached down and tapped Caspian's shoulder through her skirts. He unfolded himself from underneath her and crouched below the edge of the wagon, looking up at her.

"Did he hurt you?" His voice was so quiet and yet so harsh, she was afraid he might try to kill the man simply for intimidating her.

"No, he didn't." She shook her head. "He was just trying to intimidate me."

Caspian's voice was hard as stone. "I should kill them all for daring to hurt you."

Sophia reached down and cupped his cheek with her hand, his beard soft against her palm. "Thank you, but I just want to go," she whispered.

Caspian's jaw hardened as he nodded and slithered over the edge of the wagon. He reached up and put his hands around her waist, helping her down over the side.

They began to creep away from the wagon in the dark, and Sophia thought that they might make it to the woods unnoticed, when a cry went up from the camp behind them.

"Let's go," Caspian said, pulling her into a run, no longer concerned with being stealthy.

She could hear loud voices and her heart kicked into overdrive, her stomach threatening to boil over as she picked up her skirts and ran. The thin slippers offered no traction and she slipped more than once, holding onto Caspian's hand and allowing him to keep her from falling as they raced into the tree line.

If they were caught, Lady Manning might kill them both.

"We can't let them catch us," she said, the words coming out in heaving gasps.

Sophia wasn't surprised to find Caspian's horse tied to a tree. Her hands were clammy as Caspian put his hands around her waist and lifted her onto the horse, but he handed her the reins anyway. "Hurry," she said as she gripped the reins, her knuckles turning white.

She heard the crashing noise of men beating their way through the brush, the same noises they'd just been making themselves.

"Caspian," she cried, looking down at him.

He looked up at her, his throat bobbing as he swallowed hard.

"Run, Sophia. Don't come back," he said. Then he slapped his horse's rump, and the horse took off, heading north, heading toward safety, but leaving Caspian behind.

"Caspian," she called out as the horse continued to run, and she did her best to hold on.

How...what...she couldn't leave him.

Tears filled her eyes as she did her best to stay on the horse.

How was she supposed to leave him behind?

She turned, and in the darkness, she could barely make out Caspian's form as he pulled his blade from its sheath and prepared to fight. "Don't stop," he called out after her. "Keep going."

Sophia tried to stop the horse.

She didn't...how could she...she couldn't breathe.

How dare he try to sacrifice himself for her?

She couldn't see anything as the horse ran headlong into the darkness, with only the light of the moon filtering through the leaves. Somehow she lost the reins and she clutched the horse's mane, holding tight. She couldn't even see the reins through her tears.

Her heart broke as they ran through the woods alone.

All she could do was hang on, and pray that Caspian had help coming, and that it wouldn't be too late.

Chapter Eighteen
CASPIAN

Caspian gripped his sword as the first guard descended on him.

He prayed that Sophia would keep going.

He couldn't win against six men. His only hope was to use the forest to distract them and keep them all from attacking him at the same time. And maybe, just maybe, buy her enough time to get away.

Hopefully his brother was on his way and would find her and save her.

Even if he hadn't been in love with her, as a Royal Guard of Galamere, it was his duty and honor to fight for those in need in his country.

Rescuing Sophia seemed a fitting way to live out that duty, even if it was the last mission he would complete.

The first guard came at him with his sword drawn and Caspian threw himself into the fighting.

Every block, every blow, every moment that passed was another moment for Sophia to get farther away.

As the second and third guard descended upon him, he put his back to a tree, using it to protect his most vulnerable point, and did his best to fend them off.

Even as a sword caught his arm and sliced through his shirt, he knew that he was buying Sophia time to get away and to find help.

Would it be enough time? Did she make it away? Was she even able to stay on the horse? Had she ever ridden before?

He should have asked her. He should have invited her on a ride. He should have spent more time properly wooing her.

He should have treasured every moment they spent together.

Now, it was probably too late.

When the other three guards didn't appear, his heart sank.

Were they chasing her down?

Would his sacrifice be in vain?

Would Sophia be dragged back to Riyel anyway?

He was growing tired. Somehow, he'd managed to keep them from striking him again, but his responses were growing slower, and he could sense the anticipation in their eyes.

These men wouldn't hesitate to kill him.

There were screams and his stomach lurched.

Sophia.

But then, with screams and shouts, his brother arrived.

Men ran through the woods, lit only by the moon, and he recognized their faces. As the men fighting him turned to face their new foes, he sagged against the tree, keeping his guard up until Kellan found him and pulled him into a hug.

It took a moment to realize the hug was only a farce and Kellan was actually searching his torso for blood.

"It's just my arm," he said, and his brother let out a relieved laugh.

"You scared us," he said.

"Did you find her?" Caspian demanded.

"We have her," his brother responded, and relief hit him so hard he sank toward the ground, his legs suddenly shaking. "Whoa, whoa," Kellan said, wrapping his arm around him and pulling him back up. "Come on, let's get you bandaged up. I see you tried to make yourself a martyr so I'd have to listen to Mother sing your praises for the rest of my life, but I'd rather not have you bleed to death on me."

Caspian laughed as his brother helped him through the edge of the forest and onto the moonlit grasslands.

And there she was. His Sophia.

She sat on his horse, with two men and a slew of horses surrounding her. When she saw him, she threw herself off his horse, and he somehow found the energy to run to her.

They met in the middle, and she threw her arms around him and burst into tears.

"Don't you ever do that again, do you hear me?" she demanded, beautiful even as she sobbed into his chest.

"I don't plan on it," he said with a quiet chuckle as he pressed a kiss into her hair. "You getting kidnapped once is more than enough for me."

Sophia let out a muffled sob and he held her tightly.

"Find the woman," Caspian told his brother. "I've got Sophia."

"But does she have you?" Kellan asked. "You need your arm bandaged before it bleeds too much."

"I'll see to it," Sophia said, looking over at his brother and nodding.

Kellan disappeared, leaving the two of them alone in the moonlight.

"Your arm," she began, but he shook his head.

"It can wait a moment. I'm so sorry I left you alone at the festival, Sophia." Her name felt right on his lips.

"I don't blame you," she said softly. "I should have known better than to wander off, even if I never imagined that she would find me. I just wanted to talk to Thea."

"And I had no idea that you wouldn't be safe in our own town," Caspian said. "Clearly, we need more protection.

Sophia shook her head. "It's not your fault. It's not my fault. Neither of us could have known what would happen. All that matters is that you found me, and we're both alive, and—"

"And if she ever tries to touch you again, she dies," Caspian said, his jaw clenching.

Sophia let out a sigh and rested her head against his chest, taking a deep breath. He held her for a moment, closing his eyes and relishing the feeling of holding her in his arms.

"You didn't change your mind about us with everything that happened, did you?" he asked softly after a moment, lifting her chin with a finger to look at him, leaning down to rest his forehead against hers.

"Definitely not," Sophia said with a shaky laugh, "as long as you haven't changed your mind about me."

"All I've thought about since our last kiss is how much I wanted to kiss you again," Caspian said, tilting his face to lean in and do just that.

Her cold hands wrapped around his neck, and he closed his eyes. Tears welled up and he blinked them back as he kissed her like the world had almost ended—for them, it had.

They were alive. They were together.

And he was going to kiss her every day for the rest of his life.

He couldn't form the words yet, couldn't say anything but prayers of thanks for this moment happening after all the pain and hurt of the past twenty-four hours.

Sophia pulled away, her breath coming fast. "Thank you for saving me," she said.

Caspian leaned in to kiss her again before saying, "I will always come for you, no matter what. I will always come for you."

A tear escaped from Sophia's eyes, and he wiped it away with his thumb.

Sophia ran her hand up his arm and pain sliced through it as she touched his wound. He gasped and she pulled away, covering her mouth with her hand. "I forgot, you're bleeding," she said. "Come, we need to bandage it."

Caspian allowed Sophia to pull him toward the campfire that they had both tried to avoid earlier in the evening. There were men gathered around it again, but this time, they were on his side. They were here to help him protect his Sophia, not take her away from him.

What a difference an hour made.

As Sophia led him into the light of the fire, he could tell the bleeding had already stopped, but if she wanted to bandage him up, he had no reason to tell her no.

"Come sit," she said, bringing him to a small log next to the fire. She reached out and plucked his knife from his belt, the first person to ever get past his guard in that manner.

"I'm afraid your mother's dress is ruined," she said as she lifted the hem and used the knife to cut a small notch in the hem of her underskirt. She handed his knife back and he sheathed it as he watched her rip a strip of long white fabric to make a bandage.

He pulled off his shirt to allow her to bandage his arm and Sophia stared at his chest, her eyes widening as she took in his frame. He felt a stab of pride as she stared with no shame.

Should he tease her for looking?

Probably not, but he would definitely bring it up later.

She ran her hand down his arm to the wound, which, as he'd suspected, had already stopped bleeding. "I'm sorry you got hurt for me," she said as she began wrapping the strip of fabric around his arm.

"I'm not," he said. "I would do it all again to save you."

He couldn't tell for sure, but he could almost sense the way Sophia blushed at his words as she bound his forearm. He winced as she put more pressure on it. He would have to clean it, but that could wait until morning. For now, he would let Sophia tend to him.

His brother came into the light of the fire, pushing a bound woman before him. Hatred blazed in her eyes as she took in Sophia sitting next to him, and he resisted the urge to put himself between them.

"Of course you made friends," the woman spat out.

"They're more than friends," Sophia said, her voice ringing out, strong and true. "Meet Lords Kellan and Caspian Rendon."

Faced with the fact that they were nobility, the woman shrank slightly.

"Shall we tell them what you told me earlier?" Sophia asked. There was no menace in her voice and Caspian looked down at her in amazement. How could she be so calm?

"What, the lies I told to make you doubt yourself?" the woman snarled.

Sophia shook her head. "I don't think they're lies. I think you are telling the truth, that my father is Lord Manning, and you have stolen my title, and you kidnapped me to keep the truth from being revealed."

Caspian's eyes widened and he looked down at Sophia.

What?

Sophia was nobility?

Anger burned in him as he turned back to the woman who had kidnapped his Sophia. "We will take you to Riyel to see justice done, and the king will decide your fate. But let me be clear: whatever the king decides, if you ever touch Sophia again, you will face my wrath."

He looked at his brother and jerked his chin towards the carriage in the distance. "We will continue our journey in the morning. Until then, I want her under guard where we don't have to see her."

Kellan nodded and began barking orders to the guards as Caspian turned his attention back to Sophia.

"Is it true?" he asked her,

"I don't know," she said quietly, turning to him. "It could be. It could explain why she didn't want me where she couldn't see me, and why I always felt a connection to the portrait of Lord Manning when she forced me to clean the gallery. I just assumed it was because he had a kind face."

"Is there anyone who would know for sure?" Caspian asked gently.

If it was true...it would change everything.

"Rosaleen would know," she said softly. "But I don't know that they'll take her word against a lady's." Her voice wobbled at the end, and she closed her eyes.

Caspian wrapped his arms around her and took a deep breath. "We'll figure it out in the morning," he said soothingly. "It's been a long day, and we don't have to figure everything out tonight. Let me find you a good place to sleep," he said softly.

But she shook her head and clung to him. "Don't leave me," she said.

Caspian wrapped his arms around her even tighter. "I won't," he said. "Let's find a spot near the fire."

Dietrich approached with a stack of blankets. "Here you go," he said roughly.

When she heard his voice, Sophia let go of Caspian and whirled around. "Dietrich," she cried, immediately hugging him. "Thank you for coming for me," she said, her words muffled by his shoulder.

Caspian resisted the urge to growl at the sight of his girl hugging another man. But she quickly let go of Dietrich and returned to his side as he accepted two blankets from the pile. He would have to get used to her being friends with the man. He didn't have to like it, but Dietrich seemed like a good man, and he'd helped save them both.

"Thank you," Caspian said, reaching out to shake Dietrich's hand. "I appreciate the search party."

"Of course," Dietrich said gruffly. "What's the point of saving her from freezing to death one winter if you let her die the next?"

Sophia smiled at that, reaching over to clasp Caspian's hand in hers. "I am thankful that I was rescued in both situations."

Caspian laid out one blanket near the fire and laid down, waiting for Sophia to sit down next to him before pulling the other blanket over their laps. It was entirely improper for them to share, and his brother would surely tell their mother, but she'd asked him not to leave her, and he couldn't. Not after everything that had happened.

Dietrich laid out his blanket a few feet away on Sophia's other side and nodded to Caspian, a nod that said he would guard her other side, while somehow also warning him not to push any boundaries.

"I'll take the first watch," Dietrich said, standing at the end of his blankets.

"I'll take second," Hopkins volunteered.

Caspian hadn't even noticed he was among the rescue party, but he smiled at the guard.

"I'll take third," his brother volunteered.

Sophia looked around the circle of men who had come to rescue her, her eyes welling up with tears. "Thank you all," she said.

"Of course," Kellan said. "If you attack one of us, you attack all of us."

Caspian reached for her hand. "Let's get some sleep," he said. "We have a long ride home tomorrow, and we have many things to figure out." He laid down and she followed him, resting her head on his chest.

It felt so right.

"I can't believe you came for me," she said softly.

"Of course I did," he said, just as quietly. "I love you."

Sophia looked up at him with tears in her eyes. "I love you, too," she whispered.

With his brother lying next to him and Dietrich taking the first watch, Caspian kissed her forehead instead of kissing her properly as he would have liked to after such a declaration.

But there would be time for that.

They had all the time in the world.

Because after this, he would never let her get away again.

Chapter Nineteen
Sophia

Sophia snuggled underneath her blanket next to the embers of the fire and pretended she was still asleep. This morning was so different from the one only yesterday when she was tied to a wagon, without a blanket, freezing cold.

She could barely believe that Caspian had come for her, but he had, and she was safe.

She could hear his voice in the distance, conversing with his brother, but she curled up into a tighter ball and refused to open her eyes.

If she didn't open her eyes, she didn't have to acknowledge it was morning and face her new reality.

Was she actually the daughter of Lord Manning?

Was that why Lady Manning had hated her for so long?

Was she the heir to the estate?

Would Caspian still love her if she wasn't just Sophia?

If it was true, everything about her life would change. Would she have to move to Riyel to take care of the estate there? What would becoming a lady entail? She hadn't been raised to be a lady.

She would have to leave her goats.

And she would have to leave Caspian.

Unless he came to Riyel with her.

He'd said he loved her last night. Did he love her no matter what, even if she was now Lady Manning?

She opened her eyes the tiniest bit to see if he was in sight, but all she saw were men loading up horses.

If they were already loading horses, she should probably wake up.

She sat up and rubbed the sleep from her eyes and did her best to comb down her hair. It was a ratty, tangled mess—being kidnapped hadn't done her any favors.

She didn't need to appear perfect, but it would be nice if she looked a little less like a mess before Caspian saw her again. Not that he would stop loving her because her hair was a mess...but she didn't want to look terrible, either.

Caspian appeared a moment later, and his eyes lit up when he saw that she was awake. He hurried over to her and sat down next to her, wrapping his arm around her shoulders and pulling her close. "Good morning, my darling." He kissed her forehead. "How did you sleep?"

"So well," she said with a little laugh. "It's amazing how tired you can be after being kidnapped."

"I'm glad you were able to sleep," he said softly. "Because we have a decision to make."

"If we need to go to Riyel," she said. She didn't see any way around it. She had to find out if there was truth in Lady Manning's words.

Caspian nodded. "Are you able to go?" he asked.

Sophia took a deep breath and leaned against his shoulder. "Will you go with me?"

"Anywhere," he said.

The words brought a smile to her face, even as a new thought came to her. She looked down, unwilling to meet his gaze as she asked quietly, "Will you still love me if I'm Lady Manning?"

Caspian put his finger under her chin and lifted her face to look at him. "I wasn't lying when I said I loved you. That means I love you, no matter what your name or title is, no matter what you do. As long as you're my Sophia, I love you."

Tears came to her eyes as he leaned down and kissed her. The promise of forever love was almost more than she could bear. After searching for years for love and a family, she finally had one—and the hope of more than that, if she truly was Lady Manning.

Could she handle this much happiness in one day?

"Oh, I love you, too," she said, the words making it out around the lump in her throat.

"I suppose that's a good thing, given that I had my arm sliced open for you," he teased.

Sophia shuddered at the reminder, reaching up to touch his upper arm. "I don't want to think about that. But speaking of, how is your arm this morning?"

Caspian shrugged with his good shoulder. "It still hurts but not as badly. I'll unwrap it when we get to our mansion in Riyel and send for a healer to look at it. I'm sure all will be well."

His family owned a mansion in Riyel, too.

That made sense. And, if she was being honest, the idea of having somewhere to go to that wasn't tainted by horrible memories flooded her with relief.

He turned to her. "Unless you'd rather go to see Rosaleen right away," he said. "I should have asked and not assumed."

Sophia shook her head. "I think I'd rather go to your home."

Lord Kellan appeared, and Caspian turned to face him. "We're going to Riyel," he informed his brother.

"I'm going, too," Lord Kellan said. "I'll handle the prisoners for you. I'll have more authority."

Caspian nodded. "I'm taking Sophia home first, unless you want us there when you make your accusations."

Lord Kellan shook his head. "No, it won't be a quick process, and I'd rather give the king time to think about it and make his own inquiries before he interrogates Sophia. If there's anyone who may know for sure," he said, turning to Sophia, "can you talk to them before the king summons you?"

"Of course, Lord Kellan," Sophia said.

He shook his head. "None of that. Call me Kellan."

"I'll try to remember that," Sophia said, allowing herself a small smile.

"You're going to have to practice if it's the truth," he pointed out.

Sophia took a deep breath. He was right.

"We can cross that bridge when we get to it," Caspian said, taking her hand and squeezing it. "For now, just call him Kellan. All that lord stuff goes to his head."

Kellan shook his head. "You're one to talk. Are you ready to leave?"

"I do need a moment in the woods before we leave," Sophia said quietly.

"Of course," Kellan said. "Let me make sure it's safe first."

Sophia looked up at Caspian, her eyes wide, as Kellan made his way to the woods. Was this going to be her new normal?

"I'll get you some food," Caspian said, pulling her in for a quick hug before he released her.

By the time Sophia came back from the woods only a few moments later, the bedding was all packed up and Caspian had bread and cheese and a red apple for her.

She stared at his hands. "It's an apple."

"Yes, it is," Caspian said slowly. "Does that mean something?"

Sophia shook her head, the words sticking in her throat. "She tried to get me to eat an apple. It was how she distracted me."

"You don't have to eat it," Caspian said, pulling his hand back, but she shook her head.

"As long as you haven't poisoned or cursed it, I suppose it's safe enough to eat it."

"Absolutely no poison or curses," he said, and she reached out and took the food.

Caspian swooped her up into his arms. She shrieked as her balance disappeared and threw her arms around his neck, almost losing the food in the process.

As he began to carry her to his horse, she protested, "You don't have to carry me. I must be heavy, and your arm—"

"You're not too heavy for me," he said as he helped her onto his horse and settled in the saddle behind her. "And I'm never letting you go again."

After dispatching a man to return home and inform Lord and Lady Rendon that they were safe and they were bringing the prisoners to Riyel, Lord Kellan ordered the group to ride on. A few of the captured men rode in the cart that Sophia had been in, while at least one of the Rendon guards rode in the carriage with Lady Manning.

As they headed south, setting a fast pace, Sophia's mind whirled with all the possibilities.

Was she really a lady?

What did that mean for her future?

If she was a lady, she didn't have to work.

And if he married her, Caspian wouldn't have to find work as a guard.

It certainly would explain why Lady Manning hated her—but could it really be true?

Wouldn't someone have said something or seen a resemblance, or noticed anything about her that reminded them of her real parents?

Why hadn't anyone in the servants' hall said anything?

Wouldn't Rosaleen have hinted at something?

"Caspian," she asked after an hour of silent worrying. "Will you help me if it's true?"

"Of course," he said, squishing her for a moment in his arms. "I promise."

"Do you think it's true?" she asked softly.

Caspian took a moment before he answered. His heartbeat was a steady rhythm against her back that gave her peace, his even breathing another reminder that she was safe. "I think there's a good possibility that it's true," he said. "After you told me about Lady Manning, I asked my father if he'd known Lord Manning. He said that he had, and it was a pity when Lord Manning and his daughter had died."

Sophia's breath caught in her throat. "So he had a daughter."

"Mm-hmm."

Was it strange to talk about the man who might have been her father like he was someone she'd never met?

She had no memories of him.

How had Lady Manning managed to convince everyone that his daughter had died?

If she was in fact his daughter.

Maybe she wasn't.

Who knew?

Certainly not her.

She sighed and closed her eyes, secure and warm in Caspian's arms. "I don't suppose he said anything else about Lord Manning?"

"Only that he loved his daughter very, very much."

The words felt comforting, even though she didn't know if they were about her or not.

If she was his daughter...she had been loved. She had been cherished. And she was loved and cherished again.

Because she'd found someone who loved her for her, who had risked his life to save her, who had chased after her for miles and miles until he could bring her safely home.

It all felt like a fairytale.

She must have dozed off because the next thing she knew, they were riding through the busy streets of Riyel. Sophia's heart leaped in her throat, and she wrapped her hand around Caspian's arm as Lady Manning's home came into view.

"What's wrong?" Caspian asked quietly.

"That's it," she said as they approached the imposing residence that had been the source of her nightmares for years.

"Do you want to stop and see Rosaleen?" he asked. "Or do you want to go home and change first?"

Sophia's heart was beating faster. She'd thought she wanted time...but now that she was here, she didn't want to wait any longer to find out.

"No," she said firmly. "Let's stop."

Caspian rode up to the front steps of the mansion and dismounted. He turned and nodded to Hopkins, who brought up the rear of their entourage. "We're stopping here," he said. "Tell Kellan we'll be home in a little while."

Sophia could hardly breathe as Caspian lifted her down from his horse. She picked up the tattered and torn dress that had once looked so fine and ascended the steps while Caspian tied the reins to a fence post.

Did this home truly belong to her?

She knocked at the front door and a moment later, it opened, revealing Lady Manning's butler.

"We're not in the habit of admitting street urchins," he said blandly.

"Don't you remember me?" Sophia asked.

He looked down at her for a moment before his jaw dropped. "Sophia?"

Caspian followed her up the stairs, his presence behind her lending her strength. "I need to speak to Rosaleen," she said.

"Why didn't you come to the back door?" he said with a frown.

"Because we were already here," Caspian said in a cheerful voice. "Hello, I'm Lord Caspian Rendon."

The butler's jaw dropped again, looking between Sophia and Caspian. "Of course, come in," he said hurriedly. "Would you like to go down to the kitchen, or shall I fetch Rosaleen for you, sir?"

Sophia could feel Caspian's eyes on her, deferring to her in the moment. "We shall go to the kitchen," she said grandly, sweeping in past the butler and leading the way to the kitchen.

Nothing had changed here.

But she had changed.

When she opened the kitchen door, Rosaleen's back was turned to them. "If they didn't have any chickens today, so help me—"

She turned around and when she saw Sophia, she burst into tears. "Oh, Sophia," she said, hurrying toward them and throwing her arms around her. "You're here."

But then, perhaps realizing what that meant, she took a step back. "Oh, no. You're here. Oh, my girl, did she find you?"

Then she took in Caspian's presence, and she frowned. "And who's this, then?"

Sophia laughed. "I've missed you, Rosaleen," she said. "This is Caspian." She reached behind herself and pulled Caspian forward.

"Lord Caspian Rendon, at your service," Caspian said, bowing his head.

"Oh, my," Rosaleen said, her mouth dropping open in shock. "Sophia, my girl, what have you been up to this past year?"

"Rosaleen, I have a very important question for you," Sophia said quietly. "You're the only one I know who's been here as long as I have."

Rosaleen's eyes began to fill with tears. "It's finally happening," she said, her voice catching. "She told you?"

"That my father is Lord Manning," Sophia said, the words somewhere between a question and a statement.

Rosaleen nodded and Sophia felt faint.

It was true?

"She always was a jealous person," Rosaleen said. "She snapped up your father so quick after your mother passed, rest her soul, and as soon as your father was gone, she shoved you into my arms and announced that you had passed, too. She couldn't stand the thought that you would take her title from her, not when you were still a wee thing, and she threatened to kill you if I ever told a soul. Soon after, most folks who worked here were fired, and she replaced them all with new staff who didn't know you or your father."

"So all those times she made me clean the gallery with their portraits," Sophia mused.

"She's sick in the head," Rosaleen announced, before looking around furtively. "She's not here, right?"

Sophia laughed. "No, she's not. She's being taken to the castle by Caspian's brother where he intends to charge her with kidnapping."

Rosaleen nodded. "And once we tell them the truth about you, they can add stealing a title to her list of crimes."

There was a silence as they all took in everything that had been said. "Would you show me the gallery?" Caspian asked, reaching over to take her hand. "I'd love to see it with you."

"That's a lovely idea," Rosaleen said. "And then, child, you should change. You'll catch a cold in that dress."

Sophia smiled and gave her old friend a hug. "Thank you, Rosaleen," she said softly. "I know it couldn't have been easy for you."

Rosaleen clicked her tongue. "I'd do it all again to save you," she said, squeezing tightly. When she let go and Sophia took a step back, she saw the tears gathering in her eyes. "I can't tell you how glad I am that it's over now."

"Me, too," Sophia said, reaching out for Caspian's hand. "We're going to the Rendon family's estate, but if you don't mind, I'm sure we'll need your help to prove that I am his daughter."

"I'll be wherever you need me, my lady," Rosaleen promised.

Sophia's eyes widened at the use of a title. "That's not necessary," she said, shaking her head.

"The sooner you get used to it, the better," Rosaleen said. "Trust me, my girl."

Caspian squeezed her hand as Sophia took a deep breath. "If you say so."

She turned and looked at the door they'd come through. She wanted to go to the gallery...and she also didn't want to go.

Could she see herself walking through these hallways as the new Lady Manning?

"We don't have to go yet if you're not ready," Caspian said. "It can wait."

Sophia pondered his words for a moment but shook her head. "No. It can't."

She held his hand, and they walked through the kitchen doorway into the hallway, where the butler was waiting, a shocked expression on his face. "Welcome home, Lady Manning."

Her heart beating fast, Sophia nodded at him before passing by as she led Caspian through her home.

She was now Lady Manning, and she wouldn't let the previous holder of the title take it from her.

It was hers.

Chapter Twenty
CASPIAN

Caspian watched Sophia straighten as they walked through the Manning estate. She held herself like a lady as she led them through several hallways until they reached the art gallery, where dozens of portraits of her ancestors hung.

"They're at the end," she said softly, leading him to the end of the narrow room, where she stopped to stare up at two of the newest portraits. "Is it strange that I always thought they would like me if they'd known me?"

His heart broke for young Sophia.

Caspian stepped behind her and wrapped his arms around her, leaning down to rest his chin on her hair. "It's not strange at all," he said. "If anything, it shows that you remembered them in some way and knew how much they loved you."

"I suppose so." She sighed. "I wish I could have known them."

"I do, too," he said, "and I'm sorry for everything you went through, but I can't be sorry that your path led you to me."

Sophia turned in his arms and looked up at him. "I'm not sorry, either," she said, closing her eyes and tilting her face in expectation.

She was too short to kiss him on her own, and it was adorable.

Caspian smiled as he leaned down to meet her, giving her a short and sweet kiss before pulling back. "Now," he said, "shall we leave this place and go to my house? I want to introduce you to everyone there."

"Everyone?" Sophia asked as she took his hand and led him down the hallway again.

"We don't keep a full staff here in the city like we do at home," he said. "But there are a few folks who live here and run the estate, and we bring anyone else we need if we come."

"We didn't bring anyone this time," Sophia said. "Does that mean you'll need me to go to work?" Her brown eyes danced with amusement as she smirked up at him.

"Your serving days are behind you," he said, grinning back at her. "Now you get to be absolutely spoiled for the rest of your life."

"And who's going to spoil me?" she asked, raising her eyebrows.

"I am," he said, letting go of her hand to wrap his arm around her shoulders, tucking her into his side. "I plan on spoiling you for the rest of our lives."

"That sounds wonderful," she said softly as they made their way through the foyer.

The butler was waiting for them. "Will you be returning, Lady Manning?" he asked Sophia.

She took a deep breath, then looked at Caspian. "I think not today," she said, but there was a question in her words.

Caspian didn't know what to tell her, either. "We shall see what my brother says when he returns from the palace," he told the butler. "We may send for Rosaleen, if we need her."

"Of course, my lord," the butler said as he opened the door for them. "Good day."

Caspian led Sophia to his horse and helped her mount before untying the reins and mounting behind her. They could have walked, but he wasn't going to turn down the chance to be this close to her for a little while longer. "All this time, you were so close to me, and I had no idea," he said to her as he urged his horse forward.

"Oh?"

He nodded, though she couldn't see it. "We're merely two houses down."

She twisted her head, trying to look back at him. "Really?"

He fought the urge to laugh. "Yes. And if I'd had any idea of how she was treating you, I would have taken the door down to get to you."

"You didn't know me then," she reminded him.

"Ah, but as a member of the king's Royal Guard, I swore an oath to protect all the citizens of our kingdom. That included you, whether or not I knew you."

"But just think, if you'd barged in and rescued me there, you might not have fallen in love with me. We wouldn't have had any baby goats to knock us over and pull death defying stunts."

He grinned at the reminder of Mollie. "Yes, well, we'll just have to stop guessing what might have happened. Besides, we're here."

He dismounted and reached up to her, setting his hands around her waist and helping her down. He left his hands there a moment longer, leaning down to steal a kiss, before letting her go and turning his attention to his mount.

"Let's see if Kellan stopped by or if they are entirely unaware that we're about to barge in," he said as he gathered his reins and reached back for Sophia's hand.

"Will they be prepared?" Sophia asked anxiously as she stopped walking and pulled her hand from his. "Uninvited guests are such a hardship on the staff."

He turned to her. "It will be unexpected, but it won't be a hardship for them, I promise. We're all used to roughing it, and if they have to run to the market to buy some more food for dinner, they won't mind. No one will yell or scream if there are unwashed linens, or if there isn't a five-course dinner prepared for us."

He'd meant the words as a joke, but he could see in her eyes that he'd struck a chord.

Fury built up inside him at how Lady Manning must have treated everyone in her household for Sophia to still feel this way a year after leaving.

"Sophia," he said softly, closing the distance she'd left between them and tucking a stray lock of hair behind her ear. "They will not be unhappy to see us, I promise. If you want, we can help them prepare the food and rooms. Just come inside and meet everyone. I know they're going to love you."

She allowed him to take her hand again, and he led them to the gate that kept their home apart from the busy street. He tied his horse to the fence, then led her through the gate.

As they climbed the steps to the front entrance, Caspian tried to see their home through her eyes. Did it seem too much like Lady Manning's? All the mansions that lined this street were owned by nobility, homes for those who had estates elsewhere but needed a place to stay when they were in the city. They all looked similar—was it too similar?

He let go of her hand as he opened the front door and called out, "Rawlings, I'm home." The words echoed through the large foyer, and a moment later, Rawlings popped up.

"Lord Caspian," he said in delight. "This is unexpected."

Then his eyes took in Sophia standing next to him. "Oh, my goodness, what have you done to this poor girl?"

Caspian shook his head. "Why would you assume it's my fault? I rescued her."

"Isn't it usually your fault?" Rawlings asked, amusement glinting in his eyes.

"How dare you insinuate that I'm usually causing trouble," Caspian said, narrowing his eyes at the older man who'd cared for him during his two years in Riyel.

Sophia reached for his hand. "He didn't cause any trouble. I was kidnapped, and he saved me."

She looked up at him with love in her eyes and it took everything in him not to swoop down and kiss her senseless right in front of Rawlings.

No, he couldn't do that. "This is Lady Sophia," Caspian said, in a vain attempt to distract himself. "She's had a rough couple of days, but we're going to get it all sorted out."

"It's a pleasure to meet you, Lady Sophia. Let's get you taken care of, why don't we?" Rawlings asked, hurrying to the wall and pulling a rope. "Would you like some tea while we prepare a hot bath?"

Caspian looked down at Sophia, who suddenly appeared as if she was going to burst into tears. "Tea sounds lovely," he said. "I'll take her to the sitting room. Oh, and Kellan is here, and maybe eight other guards and men from the Northlands. They'll be arriving at some point and will need rooms as well."

"Will everyone need a bath?" Rawlings asked, showing his first sign of alarm.

"No," Caspian said. "Just this one." He reached out to take her hand and gently led her toward the sitting room. It was one of his favorite rooms in the house, where he and his brothers and his parents had spent many hours before they'd made the move to the Northlands as their usual residence. There were many happy memories here.

And now there would be more.

He sat down on a sofa and pulled Sophia onto his lap. She startled, and moved as if she wanted to slide off, but he simply wrapped his arms around her and buried his face in her neck.

Having her here, safe, in his home...it made everything that had happened start to sink in a little more. The very real danger that she'd been in, the fact that he could have been killed. "I'm so glad you're safe," he whispered, the words muffled by her skin. "I was so worried about you."

Sophia ran her hand across his hair, down the side of his face, her fingers playing with his beard. "I knew you would come for me," she said.

Her faith in him was humbling.

"I didn't know if I could save you," he admitted, "but I couldn't let you go."

She laid her head on his shoulder and took a deep breath. "I can't believe it's true."

Silence filled the room as he took a moment to let it really sink in.

Sophia, his Sophia, was nobility.

She was, most likely, wealthy.

His goat girl had turned out to be exactly what he'd been looking for all those years—and he loved her.

He'd loved her before he knew, and he would have given up the life that he'd planned for himself, but now he didn't have to.

"I'm scared," she whispered.

"It's natural to be scared," he said softly. "But I'll be right by your side, as long as you'll have me."

"Always," she said. "I'll have you for the rest of my life."

The door to the sitting room opened and two maids bustled in, accompanied by Rawlings. One maid immediately began to start a fire, while another carried a tray with tea, two cups, and a selection of dainty sandwiches.

"Oh, my goodness, that was fast," Sophia said, sliding off Caspian's lap to sit next to him.

"I told you we wouldn't be a burden," Caspian said quietly as Rawlings pulled a table over to them and the maid set the tray down on top of it.

"I hope you weren't cold," Rawlings said. "I should have started the fire myself."

"No need," Caspian said. "I could have done it if we were cold. Thank you, Rawlings."

"Your bath will be ready soon, Lady Sophia," Rawlings said.

Sophia thanked him before standing to pour them both a hot cup of tea. "I am so excited for a bath," she said as she sat back down and reached for a sandwich. "Do you think they'll have clean clothes for me?" she asked.

"I'll make sure they know to get you something from Mother's things," Caspian said, making eye contact with the maid who had finished lighting the fire. She smiled, nodded, and hurried from the room.

Sophia leaned back into the sofa, both hands wrapped around her tea, and sighed. "I can't believe we're safe."

"I can't believe you're Lady Sophia," Caspian said.

She looked over at him. "I know. It feels like a dream."

"Does it have a happy ending?" Caspian asked, scooting over to snuggle up to her.

"Yes," she said shyly, smiling up at him. "I think it does."

"I think so, too," he said, leaning down to give her a kiss.

There was a knock at the door and Rawlings poked his head in. "Your bath is ready whenever you are, Lady Sophia. I've put her in the blue room," he added, turning to Caspian. "I thought you might want her close to you."

"Thank you, Rawlings," Caspian said. Of course Rawlings would pick up on that. "Do you want to finish your tea?" he asked Sophia.

She shook her head, already setting it down. "No, I want to get out of this dress," she said. "I'll be back soon."

She followed Rawlings out and Caspian finished the sandwich in his hand before following them up the stairs to the bedrooms. He wasn't as dirty as Sophia, but he wouldn't mind a change of clothes, either.

After sponging himself off and changing, he returned to the sitting room with a drink to wait for Sophia and his brother.

His mind wrestled with the way things had changed in so short a time, and how they would change in the future.

One thing was certain: he loved Sophia and he wanted to spend the rest of his life with her.

The question was, would she want the same thing if she was no longer the goat girl? Would she still love him if she was suddenly a lady?

He mulled over the idea for the better part of an hour, until he heard the front door open as his brother arrived. There were loud, cheerful voices as Rawlings attended to the men and guards, and a moment later, Kellan walked into the sitting room.

"How'd it go?" Caspian asked, shooting to his feet.

"She's locked up," Kellan said with a sigh, sitting down in his favorite chair. "The king wants to speak to Sophia and Rosaleen tomorrow, but he liked Lord Manning and remembered his daughter, so it seems likely that justice will be done, if it is in fact true. How did you fare on that score?"

"Rosaleen says it's true," Caspian said, sitting back down, too. "So now all that's left is to convince the king of it, I suppose."

"Convince the king of what?" a beautiful voice said from the doorway.

Both men stood and Caspian couldn't stop the smile that took over his face at the sight of his Sophia.

She was wearing one of his mother's gowns, a dark green that made her pale skin and dark hair appear even more dramatic. She smiled shyly at him, and he crossed the room to her, pulling her into his arms and kissing her hair. "You look beautiful, darling," he said, releasing her to look at her again. "This dress is perfect on you."

"All your mother's doing, once again," she said with a laugh before turning to Kellan. "What news from the palace?"

"We have an appointment to see the king tomorrow," Kellan said. "He's inclined to believe it's true."

Sophia took a deep breath and reached out for Caspian's hand. "And then we can go home?" she asked.

"And then we can go home," Caspian said, squeezing her hand.

They should probably speak to the manager of the Manning estates before they did so...but he would bring that up tomorrow. He might not even be in Riyel, and they'd have to send a letter to summon him.

Rawlings came up behind Sophia and cleared his throat. "Dinner will be served in thirty minutes, Lord Kellan, if you wish to change."

Kellan nodded. "Right. I'll be back."

Caspian drew Sophia back to the sofa they'd sat on earlier. "How was your bath?" he asked with a smile.

"The most wonderful thing I've ever experienced," Sophia said with a smile. "I could get used to being a lady if that's what baths are like."

"You can have as many baths as you want," Caspian said, shaking his head at her eager expression. "If that's all it takes to make you happy."

He was just glad she no longer seemed focused on what the following day would bring. But while she may have forgotten it, he couldn't seem to stop thinking about it.

Would the king recognize her as Lady Manning? Or would the snake of a woman who'd imprisoned his Sophia for years be allowed to go free?

Could he tell that her head was buzzing like a beehive and her stomach felt like someone was churning butter in it?

Sophia could barely eat anything, only nibbling on a piece of dry toast. It wasn't until the meal was nearly over and Rosaleen was ushered into the dining room by a servant that she took a true breath, the sight of her almost-mother nearly bringing her to tears.

"Hello, my girl," Rosaleen said as she hurried over to give Sophia a hug. "Are you ready for this?"

Sophia shook her head slightly and Rosaleen smiled in sympathy. "I know, me, too," she admitted in a whisper. "What business do I have going to the palace?" she asked.

"Just as much as me," Sophia said, just as quietly.

"Have a seat, Rosaleen," Caspian said, gesturing to the seat on Sophia's other side. "Would you like some food?"

"Food that I didn't have to cook?" Rosaleen asked, grinning at Sophia. "That would be wonderful."

Caspian nodded to a servant, who immediately brought a plate for Rosaleen. They loaded it with freshly cooked eggs, two types of sausage, a biscuit, apples in honey and cinnamon, and a pat of fresh butter, and Rosaleen tucked in.

The sight of Rosaleen had calmed Sophia's nerves a bit, and she was able to eat some of the apples, the rich flavor exploding on her tongue.

But the reprieve didn't last long as Kellan stood and announced, "We'll leave for the palace shortly. Everyone is welcome to come with us. We may leave for home directly afterwards depending on what happens. Rawlings, a carriage for Lady Sophia and Rosaleen, please."

She took a deep breath as everyone in the room stood in a flurry of motion. She allowed herself to be swept along with it, following everyone out of the dining room and toward the front of the house.

The men who'd arrived with them split off, presumably going to the stables, leaving Caspian and Kellan in the foyer. "Are you ready for this?" Kellan asked her.

She shook her head and Caspian crossed the room to hold her hand.

"All will be well," he said reassuringly.

If only she could throw her arms around him and pretend that nothing was happening today that might change her life forever.

"Your carriage is ready, Lord Kellan," Rawlings said, popping up out of nowhere behind Sophia.

"That was fast," Sophia muttered.

"I took the liberty of ordering one before Lord Kellan mentioned it," Rawlings said, nodding to her when she turned to face him. "I look forward to hearing of your success, Lady Sophia."

"We'll be sure to send word," Kellan said, clapping Rawlings on the shoulder. "Thank you for preparing everything for us on such short notice. We may be spending more time in Riyel than we have in the past," he said, glancing at Sophia. "It's always good to be here."

"We are always happy to see you and your family, sir," Rawlings said, inclining his head once again.

Kellan smiled, then strode out the door as Rawlings opened it. Rosaleen followed him, leaving Caspian and Sophia in the foyer.

"Best of luck to you, Lady Sophia," Rawlings said. "I can see you've done wonders for this one here, and I look forward to you being around for many years to come." His eyes twinkled as he said the words.

Was this what it could be like when the nobility treated those in their home with respect?

"Thank you, Rawlings," Sophia said, a lump in her throat as Caspian led her to the door. "And thank you for welcoming me."

"Any guest of Lord Caspian's is welcome here at any time," Rawlings said. "I hope to see you again soon."

He closed the door behind them, and Caspian looked down at her. "I told you it wouldn't be bad," he teased.

"I wasn't concerned about visiting your family's home," Sophia pointed out. "I didn't wish to be a burden, but that wasn't the part that worried me. The worst is yet to come."

"And I'll be right by your side through it all," Caspian promised as he led her to the carriage and helped her in. "Even if it's on horseback, a few feet away from you."

Sophia laughed a little as he closed the carriage door and she watched him mount his horse through the small window, but her heart wasn't in it.

All her heart could feel was tendrils of fear snaking their way through her.

She could barely breathe as the carriage made its way deeper into the heart of Riyel.

At least Rosaleen didn't seem to expect her to talk—she was quiet, too. Perhaps worried about the fact that she would be asked to testify on Sophia's behalf.

Would the king even acknowledge testimony from a cook? Would it be enough to persuade him of her legitimacy?

"Courage, dear," Rosaleen said, squeezing her hand as they drove through the palace gates. "No matter what happens, I have a feeling you and that young man of yours will find a safe place to land."

Sophia's throat was dry, and she couldn't find the words to say, so she simply squeezed her hand and tried to take a deep breath.

It was harder than it should have been.

As their carriage stopped, Sophia let out a shaky breath, turning to Rosaleen with wide eyes.

This was it.

The moment that would set the course of the rest of her life.

The carriage door opened, and Caspian appeared. His dark eyes shone with warmth and love and his presence gave her more courage than Rosaleen's words had.

Somehow, he'd become everything she needed, without her even noticing.

He offered his hand and she placed hers in it as he helped her descend. Once she was safely on the ground, he extended his arm to her without a word. She took it, clinging to him, his steady hand only betraying how her own was trembling.

He still didn't say anything but placed his other hand on top of hers in a show of support. The warmth and weight of it stilled her shaking, and she leaned into him as he led her toward the palace steps.

Lord Kellan led the way and Sophia looked back to see that Dietrich was escorting Rosaleen, with Hopkins and another guard following behind them. The rest of the men stayed with the carriage and horses.

She turned back to gaze up at the palace. Though it wasn't the first time she'd seen it after living in Riyel most of her life, it was the first time she'd been through the gates and seen it up close.

It was much larger from here.

The thought did nothing to calm her nerves.

"Breathe," Caspian reminded her quietly as the palace doors opened before them and they were ushered inside by two palace guards.

"We have an audience with the king," Kellan said in a lofty tone.

A uniformed guard led the way down a hallway. As they walked deeper and deeper into the palace, Sophia found her nerves slowly dissipating.

It was odd, but she wouldn't complain.

The fact that it was almost over made relief swell up with every step.

Nothing she did or said would change the outcome of this visit. Surely the king had already made up his mind as to whether or not she was Lady Manning.

And Caspian had promised to love her regardless of the outcome.

She looked up at his handsome face and smiled.

Either way, she would happily spend the rest of her life loving him.

She took a true deep breath for the first time all morning and let out a sigh.

It would all be over soon.

The guard paused outside an unmarked door, one that didn't look like the entrance to a grand receiving room, which made Sophia easier. If they were merely meeting in an office of some sort, it couldn't be that bad.

Caspian gently squeezed her hand before he removed the hand covering hers. She missed the warmth immediately, but she didn't have time to be nervous as the door opened and Kellan led the way into a library.

A man poked his head around one of the shelves and said, "I'll be right with you," before disappearing again.

"Of course, Your Majesty," Kellan said, nodding his head toward nothing.

Sophia's eyes widened.

That was the king?

He looked no older than Kellan and showed no sign of pomp and royalty.

A moment later, he popped out again, and he grinned as he strode toward them with a book under his arm. "Kellan," he exclaimed. "It's been ages, my friend."

Kellan met him halfway, clasping his arm in a gesture of goodwill, bowing slightly. "It is good to see you, my king. Though I did see you only yesterday."

The king waved his hand at Kellan. "Yes, but that was in the receiving room. There's no need for formalities in here," he said. "Now, I've been having a look at the genealogies and inheritance laws." He waved the book he held.

Kellan turned to Caspian, who let go of Sophia's hand to bow. "Your Majesty," he said. "Lord Caspian Rendon, at your service."

"No need for introductions," the king said. "I know you were young when your family moved out of the city, but we were all friends as children. Please, call me Edmund."

Sophia looked between Caspian, Kellan, and the king. They'd been friends?

"I remember," Caspian admitted. "But I've been training as a member of your Guard for the past two years and it seems quite irregular to call you by your given name." He grinned.

The king sighed. "I'm sure the general would drop dead if he knew it, but I have no interest in continuing the stiff formalities of my father's rule. I wish I'd known you were in Riyel all this time. I would have looked in on you. Is that how you met the lady in question?" he asked, turning to Sophia.

His gaze was intense, and Sophia forced herself to stand straight and not shrink into herself as she dropped into a curtsey.

"Actually, I met her in the Northlands," Caspian said. "She'd run away from Lady Manning, who treated her quite terribly. It wasn't until Lady Manning went to the trouble of tracking her down and kidnapping her that we discovered there was a reason for Lady Manning's treatment of her."

The king was still looking at her.

Sophia's stomach hurt again.

"You look like her," King Edmund said quietly. "Your mother, I mean. She was young when your father married her, and she didn't mind breaking the rules to treat me like a child instead of the future king."

Sophia's mouth was dry, and she couldn't find words to speak.

"I'm inclined to believe that you're who they say you are," the king said, nodding his head at her. "Do you have any proof?"

"Only the word of the cook who was given a child to raise," Kellan said, nodding his head toward Rosaleen.

Sophia turned to see the sheer terror on Rosaleen's face, but she took a deep breath and took a step forward, bobbing an awkward curtsey as she did so. "Lady Manning brought her stepdaughter to me a day after Lord Manning died. She told me that if I told anyone Sophia's true parents, she would kill both of us, and I knew I couldn't let that happen. I began calling her by her middle name and did my best to teach her all the things she would need to know. But Lady Manning was cruel to her, and it became clear that she was worried about someone recognizing Sophia for who she truly is. She is Lady Blanche Sophia Manning, Lord Manning's daughter and heir."

King Edmund nodded gravely. "Thank you for your testimony." He crossed his arms across his chest as he turned to stare at Sophia. "And what about you?" he asked. "Do you believe it's true?"

Sophia nodded. "If I may be honest, Your Majesty, I didn't truly believe it myself until we visited the art gallery at the mansion yesterday. But when I saw the portraits of my parents, knowing they were most likely my parents...I couldn't deny it any longer."

"She looks just like them," Caspian said. "I almost thought the portrait of her mother was Sophia herself."

The king nodded and smiled at Sophia. "I hereby declare you to be the heir of the Manning estates, Lady Sophia Manning. Your stepmother will find that the punishment for hiding a child's true parentage to gain a title is quite steep unless you wish it to be reduced."

Sophia's eyes widened. He was giving her the choice? She didn't want to have to make that decision. She turned to Caspian, who could sense her indecision and reached for her hand.

"I think Lady Sophia will agree with whatever you see fit," he told the king, and Sophia nodded.

"Would you like to be here when I speak to her?" the king asked.

A chill ran down Sophia's spine at the thought of seeing Lady Manning again.

But no.

She wasn't Lady Manning.

Sophia was now Lady Manning.

And being there was probably the proper thing for a lady to do, right?

"As long as you'll stay with me," she told Caspian.

"Always," he said with a smile.

It wasn't the first time he'd said that, but it still made her smile.

Always was a long time.

The king nodded to Kellan. "Would you tell the guards outside to bring her to the throne room?" he said. "I think the occasion warrants it."

Kellan laughed as he walked away, and King Edmund turned to Sophia with a grin. "Shall we adjourn to the throne room, Lady Sophia?"

Sophia hid her smile as she nodded. "As you wish, Your Majesty."

Chapter Twenty-Two
Caspian

Caspian followed King Edmund toward the throne room, Sophia's hand tucked into his arm. Even though he'd had some time to adjust to the idea of Sophia being nobility, it hadn't felt like it would change much. But now that it was true, now that the king had recognized her as Lady Manning...it was all crashing into him.

His Sophia was Lady Manning, with lands and people to look after and provide for.

And she knew nothing about being nobility. But he did—and he would be there to help her shoulder the burden. If she was willing for him to do so.

Her skirts swished around them as they walked, and he looked down at her with a smile. The dark blue dress she wore this morning belonged to his mother, and despite being made for someone else, it fit Sophia well. It was shorter on his mother, of course, but the way it brushed the floor as Sophia walked made her look like a lady on her way to attend a ball.

Sophia had probably never been to a ball.

They would have to throw one for her.

She held her head high as they made their way into the throne room. Caspian looked around, trying to see it through her eyes. What would she think of the glittering drama of the royal throne room?

King Edmund made his way up the dais and settled on his throne, gesturing for their party to stand off to the side.

Sophia began to tremble as they waited for the former Lady Manning to be brought before the king. If only he could pull her into his arms and tell her all would be well—but he didn't want to undermine this, her first moments as nobility. She was strong enough for this.

The doors to the throne room were thrown open and she froze as her stepmother was brought into the room, her upper arms held by two guards. The woman was wearing the same gown they'd captured her in, a gaudy purple thing that seemed designed to highlight the fact that she was wealthy. His mother's dresses were far simpler and much more to Caspian's taste. He resisted the urge to look down at Sophia, as if he hadn't already practically memorized the way she looked in his mother's gown.

She looked noble, and the clothes weren't necessary to highlight that. They simply served to showcase it.

"Your Majesty," the former Lady Manning began as she was brought before the king.

King Edmund showed no sign of softening toward her as he simply waited.

Caspian felt a surge of satisfaction at how desperate the woman looked.

She deserved it for her treatment of his Sophia.

"What have I done to deserve such treatment?" the woman asked, attempting to wrench her arm away from the guard. "I am Lady Manning, your Majesty's loyal servant, and I have been treated rudely since the moment I arrived."

Her focus was entirely on her sovereign. Had she even noticed Sophia was in the room?

"Do you know what charges have been brought against you?" King Edmund asked, his voice hard. Gone was the childhood friend they'd met in the library. Here, he was every inch the king that he'd become.

"I cannot imagine what they might be," the woman said airily.

"You have been charged with kidnapping and attempting to steal a child's title from them," the king said.

"Stealing a title?" She laughed. "What a story. The only title I have is one that I was given through my marriage, certainly not any that were stolen."

"And what of your stepdaughter, Lady Blanche?" the king asked.

Her face grew somber. "A tragedy to lose both my husband and our daughter so quickly after each other," she said, sniffling. "I cannot imagine you would understand the pain, Your Majesty."

"I know what it is to have someone you love taken from you," the king said. "What I don't understand is how you could then take away his daughter's inheritance."

"I'm afraid I don't know what you mean," the woman said, but her voice held a tremble that hadn't been there before.

"You don't?" the king asked. "Perhaps I should refresh your memory. Where is the cook?"

The blood drained from the former Lady Manning's face as Rosaleen emerged from the back of their group.

"Do you still deny knowledge of what you've done?" King Edmund asked.

The woman didn't answer as her gaze slid to Sophia.

Caspian let his hand rest on top of hers where she clutched his arm.

"Do you deny it?" King Edmund asked again, his voice louder now.

"I have only ever done what is best for the Manning estate," the woman screeched, venom in her voice as she flung the words at Sophia. "She would have run it into the ground long before its time."

The king nodded grimly. "So it's true. And instead of owning up to your treason and apologizing, you choose to pretend as if it never happened. You are not repentant, and I have no inclination to treat you accordingly. You are hereby stripped of your title, your wealth, and your lands, and they will be restored to the rightful owner."

"I am the rightful owner," she began to say, but King Edmund shook his head.

"As for you, the punishment should fit the crime. You are hereby sentenced to as many years of service as you forced the rightful Lady Manning to endure. Though I've no doubt that you'll find more leniency in your servitude than you granted to Lady Sophia."

"You ungrateful wretch," the former Lady Manning hissed, turning to Sophia and Caspian with hatred in her eyes. "I'll have you all killed for this."

"I don't suppose death threats toward nobility come with an additional sentence," Kellan said lightly from his place beside Caspian.

The king turned to them with a mischievous glint in his eyes. "You are right, Lord Kellan. I don't take threats to my favorite members of court lightly."

Caspian fought the urge to grin. Maybe he should have told Edmund sooner that he'd been serving in the guard for the past two years. He'd assumed that being king would have changed him, but he was still the good friend he'd remembered from his childhood.

"Lady Sophia, how many years did you spend as a servant in your own household?" the king continued.

Sophia turned to Rosaleen.

"Twenty, Your Majesty," the cook answered.

The king nodded. "I think we'd best double the sentence. And to make it easier to remember, I think it best to bring the number of years to fifty."

She opened her mouth to protest, and King Edmund cut her off. "And if you don't wish to serve for fifty years, I could be convinced to make it fifty years in the dungeon. Is that your wish?"

She shook her head and King Edmund nodded regally. "Do you have anything to add, Lady Sophia?"

Sophia stared steadily at the woman who had held her captive for so many years. "I wish you peace," she said. "Your heart has long been twisted by wickedness. I hope that as you live out your sentence, you may find peace and comfort."

Caspian looked down at the woman he loved. How could she be so forgiving? He certainly wasn't. If anything, he thought Edmund's sentence was light after the years of pain she'd put Sophia through. But he wouldn't complain. As a member of the Royal Guard, he knew that prisoners who chose to work out their sentences instead of languishing in the dungeons were highly guarded and had no opportunity to cause trouble.

And right now, that's all he wanted—to have peace for the rest of their lives.

The former lady was led away by the guards and Caspian turned to Edmund with gratitude coursing through his veins. "Thank you," he said simply.

"Of course," the king said, smiling at him and Sophia. "I always love the opportunity to see justice done—even more so when it's on behalf of a friend. Please let me know if you choose to stay on as a member of the Guard. I would welcome the chance to have you closer."

Caspian looked down at Sophia and released her grip on his arm to take her hand in his. "I am considering resigning, but I will let you know my final decision." He turned to his sovereign. "Whatever the outcome, I am thankful for the honor of serving in your Guard for the past two years, my king."

"I am proud to have had you as a member," King Edmund said. "I'm sure you have many things to do, but please, send word when you are in Riyel again. I would love to invite you all to dinner."

"Thank you, Your Majesty," Sophia said softly. "For all of it."

"I cannot wait to watch your return, Lady Sophia," the king said, nodding his head to her.

Sophia squeezed Caspian's hand and looked up at him. "Can we go home now?" she whispered.

Caspian grinned. "Yes, we can go home."

They left Riyel quickly, only stopping to leave Rosaleen and collect the books from Lady Manning's study so they could look them over and determine the stability of the estate. While it would have been easier to do it in Riyel, and they should have spoken to the estate managers, he could tell that Sophia needed to go back to the Northlands, if only for a few days.

She needed time to adjust to her new normal, and taking her home to his family would give her that.

It had nothing to do with the fact that he wanted his father and brother's help in looking over the books for the first time.

Sophia rode in his family's carriage as they made their way to the inn that marked the halfway point in the journey to Riyel. When they stopped overnight, it struck Caspian that this was the first of many journeys to the Northlands together.

He'd grown up making this journey regularly before their family relocated to make the Northlands their main home. Now it seemed, at least for the time being, he would be back in Riyel.

But this time, it wouldn't be because of his parents, or because he was in the Guard, but because of the woman he loved.

The following morning dawned bright and the sun shone as they made their way home. Caspian smiled when the road split between the town and his father's estate.

They were almost home.

He could hear the cry that went up when the guard standing watch spotted them, and there was a great hullabaloo as they rode into the courtyard. Before they had even come to a stop in front of the house, Lord and Lady Rendon were rushing out to meet them.

When she saw them, Lady Rendon clapped her hands over her mouth, and she hurried to him with tears in her eyes. "Oh, my love," she said as Caspian swung down from his saddle.

He hurried to open the carriage door for Sophia, helping her out, and his mother immediately pulled Sophia into her arms for a hug. "I'm so glad you're safe. I was so worried about you."

Lord Rendon clapped Caspian on the back. "Good job saving her, son," he said.

The guards took the horses toward the barn and Sophia turned to watch them go. "Are my goats well?" she asked.

Caspian tried not to laugh. She'd been kidnapped and discovered she was a lady and the first thing she asked about when she arrived home was the goats.

"Yes, the stable master took good care of them while you were gone," Lady Rendon said with a smile.

Liliana barreled out of the house and ran to him, throwing her arms around him. "I'm so glad you're back," she said.

"How did your business in Riyel end?" Lord Rendon asked with a meaningful look at Kellan.

"I would be honored to introduce you to Lady Sophia Manning," Kellan said, nodding respectfully in Sophia's direction.

She blushed as everyone in the courtyard turned to stare at her.

The news would spread like wildfire through the estate.

Liliana's eyes widened and her mouth dropped open. "You're a lady?" she asked.

"I am," Sophia said quietly. "Though I don't know much about it. Will you help me?" she asked.

"Of course," Liliana said, hurrying over to give her a hug, too.

After Liliana let go, Caspian stepped forward and took Sophia's hand in his. "The woman who stole her title and kidnapped her three days ago has been sentenced to fifty years of labor by the king, and Sophia has been given the title that was rightfully hers."

His mother turned to him. "This is why you were asking about Lord Manning, isn't it?"

He grinned. "You've found me out. I had no idea this would be the case when I was asking, however. I simply wanted to know more about the woman who'd mistreated Sophia."

"And now justice has been served," Kellan said.

"I told Sophia we would help her," Caspian said. "We stopped and got the books for her estate so we could look them over with her. If the former Lady Manning was willing to steal a title that wasn't hers, I don't know how well she looked after the estate."

"Of course we'll help," Lord Rendon said.

"Come inside," Lady Rendon said, reaching for Sophia and ushering her toward the manor. "There are so many things to do, and we'll be here to help you with all of them."

"I can't wait," Liliana said, taking Sophia's hand.

Sophia looked back at him with a smile as she followed his mother and sister into the manor. He let her go, knowing she was in capable hands.

He had something he needed to say without her hearing it.

"I want to marry her," he told his father and brother as soon as they were safely away. "I wanted to marry her before I knew, but now that this has happened, she needs my help."

"You should talk to your mother about that," his father said. "That's her domain."

"I wasn't asking for advice about marriage," Caspian said. "I was wondering if you had any advice on helping her rebuild her estate. The mansion in Riyel looked as if it had been stripped of most of its decor, and there were barely any servants. I'm assuming any other properties will have issues, too."

"We'll look over the books," his father promised.

"And you know we'll be here to help with anything," Kellan said.

"It's not like you've got any pressing needs of your own to take care of," Lord Rendon told his oldest son, narrowing his eyes.

"I'll find a wife when I'm ready," Kellan said. "How did this get turned on me? Caspian's the one who wants to marry a newly found lady whose estates are most likely in poor shape."

"And Gideon likes to disappear for days or weeks at a time," Caspian pointed out helpfully.

His father sighed. "Gideon is a problem I'll have to deal with. But first, you two."

"First, Caspian," Kellan said firmly.

"Yes, please," Caspian said with a grin. "Now if you don't mind, I'm going to go find Sophia and make sure Mother isn't scaring her."

"She'll have to get used to Mother if you marry her," Kellan pointed out as Caspian hurried toward the house, ignoring his brother's helpful advice.

Yes, she would have to get used to his mother, but he truthfully wasn't worried about it.

He was worried about making sure she knew he would be there for her, no matter what.

He had to bide his time, waiting through dinner and an evening in the sitting room with his family, discussing everything that had changed. But once his mother had sent Liliana to bed, he stood and snagged Sophia's hand. "Come walk with me?" he asked, and he was rewarded with a smile.

"Always," she said.

"Goodnight," his mother said with a knowing smile as he towed Sophia out of the room.

"Goodnight, Mother," he called back.

He led the way out of the manor into the courtyard. The darkness hugged them as a cool breeze blew past. Sophia instinctively moved closer to him, and he wrapped his arm around her waist as she shivered.

"I should have brought my cloak," she said lightly as they made their way to the same fence where they'd sat under the stars not that long ago.

"I'll keep you warm," he said, pulling her to a stop and pulling her into his arms.

"You are good at that," she said. He could hear the smile in her voice as she buried her face in his chest. "I'll keep you around, if only so my nose isn't cold ever again."

Caspian laughed as she made a show of rubbing her nose against his shirt. "Well, you're the perfect height for me."

She looked up at him with a twinkle in her eyes. "No, I'm far too short. It's rather convenient for cold noses, however."

"I see, you only keep me around because I'm convenient," he teased.

"No," she said, her voice turning serious. "You're more than convenient, Caspian. You're perfect for me, and I hope you know how much I love you."

"Even if your title is better than mine now?" he asked as he leaned down and dropped a kiss on her hair.

"Especially now," she said. "Before, I worried that I wasn't good enough for you. Now I still worry that, but now I know how desperately I need you—not just for me, but for the estate that I'm responsible for managing. I don't know the first thing about running an estate of my own or being a lady. I don't know how to do any of this without you."

"Oh, I see, you used to love me for me, and now you only love me for my title."

"That's not what I meant," she protested, laughing when she saw the teasing glint in his eyes. "You know that's not what I meant."

"I know," he said, pulling her even closer, closing his eyes, and taking a deep breath. "I think you and I were meant for each other."

"I should hope so," she said, "given that I have no intention of ever letting you go."

Caspian grinned. "So how do you feel about me calling you Blanche?"

She shuddered. "Please don't."

Caspian laughed and held his Sophia tight. "What about 'love of my life'?"

Sophia thought about it for a moment, the corners of her mouth turning up in a smile. "I think I could get used to that one."

"I think I could, too," Caspian said.

He leaned down to kiss her, all the words he didn't know how to say wrapped up in the moment.

He had the rest of their lives to figure out the right words to say. For now, kissing her was easier.

EPILOGUE

Caspian made his way into the study and found Sophia with his mother, curled up in a ball on the couch reading a book. She smiled at whatever she was reading, and joy spread through him at the sight of her enjoying herself.

"Sophia," he said softly. She looked up and immediately closed her book when she saw him. "Come with me?"

"Of course," she said, taking his hand and following him out into the courtyard.

She stumbled on a rock, and he caught her, swinging her into his arms with ease.

"My hero," she said, wrapping her arms around his neck.

Sophia had adjusted to living in the manor extremely well. She still checked on the goats, and she was in the process of teaching someone else how to make butter and the goat milk soap that apparently the whole town was talking about.

But in the past couple of weeks since learning that she was Lady Manning, they'd spent more time with his family, going over the books for her estate and teaching her what everything meant.

Despite his fears after visiting the mansion in Riyel, overall, the estate was fairly well off. The steward of the country estate had done well, creating enough profit with the crops they raised to subsidize the former Lady Manning's extravagant spending.

They should visit the estate themselves...but there was something Caspian wanted to do first.

Propose.

As it was, he had no weight when it came to the Manning estate. But as Sophia's betrothed, he would be able to stand by her side and help her.

His stomach twisted as he waited for Kellan to set the next part of his plan into motion. He'd spent most of the past weeks thinking of the best way to propose to Sophia...and hopefully it would all work.

As Sophia's favorite goat ran out of the barn toward them, excited to see her favorite person, he took a deep breath.

It was time.

"Oh, look, Mollie's out." He set Sophia on her feet, facing the stable.

"Hi, baby," Sophia exclaimed. "What's that on her neck?" she asked, not really expecting him to answer. She crouched in the dust of the courtyard, not caring that she was wearing another one of his mother's dresses. "It's a box," she exclaimed, untying the ribbon and pulling it off of Mollie's neck before tucking the baby goat under her arm to keep her from running away.

She tried to open the box with one hand and Caspian said, "Here, allow me."

His mouth was dry, his hands were sweaty, and he could barely breathe, but he couldn't lose momentum now.

He took the box from her and opened it, dropping to one knee as he did so.

Sophia's eyes widened and she let out a tiny squeal, clutching Mollie tightly.

He swallowed hard and forced his voice to work. "I love you, Sophia. I know we've only known each other for a few months, but you complete me. You're the first thing I think of when I wake up, and the last thought every night before I fall asleep. I want to spend the rest of my life with you, and I promise to treasure you for the rest of our days. Will you do me the great honor of becoming my wife?"

Sophia squealed again, then clapped her hand over her own mouth. "Sorry," she said in a muffled voice.

Did that mean she accepted? His heart was beating impossibly fast.

The other goats appeared in the courtyard, causing a commotion at the stable door, and Sophia's attention turned to them. "Did someone let all of them out?" she asked, staring at the goats.

"I'm still kneeling here," Caspian pointed out. "Was that squeal supposed to be a yes?"

"Oh, no, I'm so sorry, yes," Sophia exclaimed, putting Mollie down to throw her arms around his neck. Her exuberance was more forceful than he was prepared for, and they fell, toppling to the ground. "Oh, no," Sophia said, struggling to sit up and doing her best to pull him with her. She began brushing dirt off his shoulder. "I'm sorry, I didn't mean to get you dirty."

Caspian sat up, wrapping his arm around her waist as she perched on his legs. "As long as it's with you, I don't mind getting a little dirty."

One of the goats started nuzzling his shoulder and he shrugged, attempting to shake the goat off.

As long as they didn't try to lick his hair, he'd be fine.

Sophia's eyes widened. "Where's the man who was afraid to walk through the goat pen?" she teased. "He's the one I fell in love with."

"He climbed onto the barn roof to save your baby goat and realized you were worth a little dirt and grime. After all, as you've reminded me more than once, baths exist."

Sophia leaned forward, taking his face in her hands and planting a kiss on his lips. "I love you, Caspian Rendon."

"I love you, too." He brushed her hair out of her face, tucking it behind one ear. "You know that, right?"

"I do," she said.

One of the baby goats attempted to chew on Sophia's dark hair and he gently batted it away.

Sophia's smile was dazzling, and he resisted the urge to lean down and kiss her again.

"Stop distracting me," he said, shaking his head at her. "Let me get this ring on you before we lose it to one of the goats."

Sophia laughed and gave him her hand. "It's beautiful," she said, staring down at the large emerald that he slipped onto her finger.

"I'm glad you think so," he said. "I wrote to Rosaleen and asked if there were any rings that your mother had left behind, and she told me this was the ring your father proposed with. I thought you might like to wear it, too."

Tears filled Sophia's eyes and his widened. "No, don't cry," he said, reaching up to wipe away her tears. "This is supposed to be a good thing. If you don't like it, I can get you one of your own."

"They're happy tears," Sophia said, looking down at the ring on her finger and sniffling. "Thank you. You knew how much I would love this, even though I didn't have a clue."

Relief poured through him.

She'd said yes. She loved the ring. Nothing had gone wrong.

There was a slamming sound as the manor door opened and his sister burst into the courtyard, his parents following her. Kellan appeared in the stable doorway, looking very pleased with himself for playing his part. Hopkins turned around from where he'd been pretending not to eavesdrop while posted at the manor's gate, and Cook's smiling face appeared around the corner of the manor.

"She said yes," Caspian exclaimed as his sister rushed at the two of them.

"I knew she would," Liliana said, throwing her arms around both of them. "Now we can throw an engagement ball, and Mother said I'm old enough to attend!"

Sophia let out a nervous chuckle. "Must we?"

"We must," Lady Rendon said cheerfully as the rest of his family approached them.

Kellan offered Sophia a hand and helped her to her feet before pulling Caspian up as well.

"But don't worry," his mother continued. "You'll have Caspian by your side through it all."

"Yes, I will," Sophia said, smiling up at him as he wrapped his arm around her waist and pulled her close.

"Does this mean you'll be moving to Riyel?" Liliana asked.

"We'll have to go for a while," Caspian said, "but we'll definitely come back to visit, and maybe someday we'll build an estate out here, too."

"And we can always visit Riyel more," Lady Rendon said as she gave them both a hug. "Visiting the city is much more appealing when I have someone I love there."

"I was there for two years and you didn't visit," Caspian protested.

Lady Rendon smiled. "I meant Sophia," she said sweetly.

Liliana grabbed his elbow. "I think you should have a home here, too. And then, when you have children, I can play with them."

Caspian smiled at his sister, but his mind was running wild with images of children running around with Sophia's dark hair and his eyes.

Yes, he could imagine bringing his children here, and when he looked at Sophia, he knew she was thinking of it, too.

Mollie jumped up on Sophia's leg, letting out a loud noise as she begged for attention.

"I'll miss Mollie though," Sophia said.

Caspian rolled his eyes, but he smiled down at the little goat. "We can bring Mollie with us, if Liliana can spare her. And if she can't, I'll get you some goats of your own."

Sophia reached up and pulled him down to kiss him again. "I think we're going to be very happy," she said with a smile. "You, me, and our goats."

This wasn't the future he'd imagined when he came home, but there was nothing else he'd rather have. "You, me, and our goats," he agreed.

Thank you so much for reading Once Upon An Apple! If you loved it, I would be honored if you left a review on Goodreads, Amazon, or BookBub – reviews help indie authors more than you can know!

To read a bonus epilogue showing Sophia and Caspian's engagement ball in Riyel, visit

chickadeelanepress.com/apple-epilogue.

ONCE UPON A ROSE

BEATRICE'S STORY CONTINUES IN Once Upon A Rose!

A cursed lord, a librarian, and their disguised dragon pet.

Being the first librarian in their small town is everything Beatrice Montgomery has ever dreamed of–except no one in town knows what to make of her, or the library. But spending her days surrounded by books is an occupation beyond her wildest dreams, and she'll do whatever it takes to make the library a success.

Lord Alexander Dunham's time is running out. Providing for his estate and the people dependent on him before his curse ruins his life is his first priority--and that means he needs a wife, immediately. Proposing a marriage of convenience to the prim librarian seems like the perfect plan: he gets a wife, she gets funds for her library, and the sorcerer trying to steal his estate gets nothing.

Even with his lips sealed about the curse, a transforming dragon pet watching his every move, and a wife who's winning over everyone on their estate, their marriage of convenience should have solved all of Alexander's problems. Unfortunately, he's falling for his wife, and it's causing a new problem: he's no longer willing to die. Can Alexander and Beatrice outwit the most powerful sorcerer in the Northlands, or will Beatrice lose the man she's growing to love?

Once Upon A Rose is a Beauty and the Beast fairytale retelling and the second book in the Galamere Chronicles. Each standalone book is a retelling of a beloved story or fairy tale, with the swoon-worthy sweet romance of a Hallmark movie, the wholesome and heartwarming feeling of cozy fantasy, and the comfort of a found family of friends, with a sprinkling of danger and a dash of magic.

AUTHOR NOTE

THANK YOU SO MUCH for reading Once Upon An Apple!

I grew up with goats and being the "goat girl", but this is the first time I've ever gotten to write them into a book. I loved writing this book, and I hope you loved Caspian, Sophia, and their seven goats as much as I did.

I also grew up in a large family with a lot of love, and I hope that came across in Caspian's family.

If you're wondering how Thea and Ginger came to be at the Cozy Cat Café, you can find their story in Once Upon A Café, and Beatrice's story will continue in Once Upon A Rose!

You can learn more about upcoming books in the world of Galamere by joining my newsletter at chickadeelanepress.com/newsletter, or following me online—I'm @LandiWrites in most places! I'd love to meet you around the internet!

Wishing you cozy books, warm drinks, and fluffy books,
Gabrielle

ALSO BY GABRIELLE LANDI

Once Upon A Café

Join Thea and Ginger as they start the Cozy Cat Café in this cozy fantasy novella from a cat's POV.

Hosta Falls
Sweet Contemporary Romance Series

If you enjoyed the found family feels, small town vibes, and sibling banter of Once Upon An Apple, you may also enjoy Gabrielle Landi's Hosta Falls books, a contemporary romance series with just kissing.

ACKNOWLEDGEMENTS

Coming back to cozy fantasy felt like coming home, and I wouldn't have been able to do it without the encouragement of Sush and the MIF crew. I'm so thankful that you encouraged me to QTP and go back to something I truly loved.

And while I wouldn't have started without those folks, I wouldn't have gotten it published without my beta readers and editor! Ariel, Erin, Krysten, Kaitlyn, Larisa, and Rebekah, your feedback was so helpful in shaping Once Upon An Apple—I hope you like the new ending! Bethany, without your feedback and texts at all hours of the night, this book would look drastically different—I'm so glad we're "cousins"! And Lisa, your edits are always so helpful and fast and I appreciate you so much!

I could not have made this book the gorgeous book that it is without running a Kickstarter campaign. Anthea and the Kickstarter for Authors group—you were incredibly encouraging, and I'm so thankful that I found you.

And my Kickstarter backers! Without you, we would not have been able to get the stunning map that's in the front of this book, or the art of Sophia and Caspian and our gorgeous illustrated hardcover. You have no idea how much your support means to me. My eternal thanks and gratitude to you, my Kickstarter friends!

While some of them chose to not have their name printed, I want to give a special shoutout to all of them, including Amanda Balter, Amanda McGee, Amanda Thompson, Annie Sullivan, Barbara Meijsen, Becky B, Billie Humphrey, Billye Herndon, Cassandra Stubbs, Charlotte P., Chautona Havig, Cherelle H, Chloe Griffith, Darci Cole, The Dickinsons, Eileen S., Elle Steward, Elvina Patino, Faye Quinn, Franchesca Caram, Gianna Christopher, Grammy Jonas, Grandma Mechura, Hannah W., Heiko Koenig, Jean Knight Pace, Jennifer Daniels, Jennifer Kieran, Katherine Malloy, Kathryn M., Keri K, Kimmy, Laura WB, Leah Outten, LJF, Lucy Dembski, M. Corso, Magaidh and Teresa Bussell, Megan Astell, Michelle Meyering, MichelleG, Momma Lisa, Renee Mandrink, Robyn S, Serena, Shannon Mechura, Stacy Ward, The Freeman Family, Victoria Psomiadis, and Virginia Crocker. You all helped change my publishing career, and I will be forever grateful.

Ireen Chau and Cartographybird made my first time commissioning art for my writing an incredible experience, and I'm so thankful for the hard work they both put into the art in this book!

OUAP and FaRoFeb, thank you for being there to answer all of my questions, squeal about my successes, and encourage me to keep going. I'm so thankful for author friends like you!

And finally, a huge thank you to my family. Your support keeps me going and I love you all so very much! <3

ABOUT THE AUTHOR

Gabrielle Landi lives in Southern Indiana with her husband and children and has a soft spot for every stray cat that ends up on her front porch. When she's not writing, she spends her time chasing children, wishing there was more coffee, and eating chocolate like it's her job. If she had to write her own love story in tropes, it would include second chance romance and a secret relationship, and would be entirely unbelievable.

Follow online at:

ChickadeeLanePress.com
Facebook: Author Gabrielle Landi
Instagram: @LandiWrites
TikTok: @LandiWrites